Theresa Spearman Ovbije

RESURRECTION
FROM THE FLOODS

... OLD THINGS PASS AWAY ...

ISBN-10: 098570201X
ISBN-13: 9780985702014

Spearman Ovbije International Leadership Foundation (SOIL)
Publisher
P.O. Box 966
Clarkston, GA 30021

DEDICATION

This book was birth by God. My husband Reverend L.O. Ovbije, was catalyst to consistently and persistently nudged me to complete this work. In the end, the entire experience was meant to support others in their quest to complete a literary work. Our sphere of possibilities is expanded when ideas and thoughts are shared through literary expressions and reflections.

I give honor and thanks to my mother Alice C. Spearman, who is in heaven and among that great cloud of witnesses. She always encouraged all of her children to keep climbing.

I also hope this work encourages my nieces, Kristin Mary Alice Kenner and Alexandria Renee Livingston and our precious little cousin Delon Esther Hall, to pursue big dreams and trust God to bring them to pass.

To my sisters Pat Livingston and Regina Kenner whom I love dearly and who love me unconditionally.

ACKNOWLEDGMENTS

Many people had faith in me even when, at times, faith in myself waned. Encouraged by expressed confidence in my talents, people obeyed God and let Him use them to remind me of my faith and resolve to live a life of purpose.

CONTENTS

CHAPTER 1

PEACE, PEACE THEN SUDDEN DESTRUCTION

The cherry blossoms in Washington, D.C. always excited visitors to the city and if the truth be told, it was "eye candy" for residence as well. Without question however, it meant super business for *The Monet Gardens Restaurant* of Georgetown.

For Rita, the owner of The Monet Gardens, the joy and excitement of spring came on multiple levels. The boom in business was a wonderful indicator of the arrival of the spring season. Then there was a sense of security in the spring, no hurricanes, no hazardous weather warnings and no floods. Even though Washington rarely experienced, "evacuation" or hazardous weather conditions, spring for Rita was a season of relief. Since "Katrina", relief, peace and safety were precious commodities and not to be taken for granted.

However, on this particular spring morning, strong winds of change were afoot. Rita moved anxiously, from her car, reflecting on the news from New York. Her executive chef accepted a position at the Ritz properties in New York. As she calculated the blow of Mark's departure from The Monet 2 of NY, Rita's movements were more brisk. The news definitely affected her plans to establish Monet 3 in Toronto, Canada the next year.

Rita entering the restaurant with anxiousness and an air of irritability, calling for Chad, the executive chef at the Monet of Georgetown. In

1

Washington, everyone affectionately referred to the Monet as a cornerstone of elegance, where politicians, power brokers and beautiful people wined and dined.

Amanda, Rita's executive assistant, was already doing business on the phone as Rita breezed through the reception area. Amanda made eye contact and nodded slightly. Amanda knew Rita well, so she knew something was brewing. Nevertheless, her focus was on arranging accommodations for Congressman Wade from Georgia and his party of ten.

"Yes, I've confirmed a party of ten, a week from this Saturday. Please let the Congressman know we are delighted we could accommodate him this time. We appreciate your patience. Yes, I am very familiar with Reverend Blake, in Atlanta; I watch his ministry all the time. I am looking forward to him visiting our city. Yes, please call me directly if you need to make any changes."

Chad appearing in the doorway of the kitchen entrance, responded with his usual calm demeanor, "Rita, my beloved, what happened to the cheerleader this morning? Where is my kumbyie, high five, you're brilliant, good morning, you're the man, Chad?"

"Chad, … Mark is leaving and going over to the Ritz properties. I should be glad for his good fortune but this really puts a wrench in our expansion plans. And I'm sorry Chad, good morning."

"Rita, I told you Mark was an egotistical, self serving, "wanna be" brilliant chef, so what else is new?"

"Chad, you know that whole operation in New York is the stepping stone into Canada". Mark, bless his heart, was very brilliant and very Canadian. And Chad, you never really worked with me on the whole teaming effort."

"Rita, it amazes me how smart you are, yet you're so naïve about people. Mark wants what he wants. Your plans didn't mean sh…. sorry I mean cramp to him. But don't feel bad, Ritz won't keep him very long either. Mark is out to rule the world. But don't fret my sweet Rita, I got you covered. I'll just take up residence in New York for a couple of months and scout out some prospects to replace Mark. You can continue your plans to take Monet international."

" Chad I knew you were wonderful but this makes you a precious soul. So, what about things here? I didn't think you were in the business of cloning."

"What makes you think I'm not? You know Josh and Claudette? You rave about them all the time. If I weren't secure, you would have a problem with me. Well, they've been waiting, patiently I might add, to spread their wings. I think this temporary shift will give them that opportunity."

" Chad, they're pretty young, can they handle it and more importantly, can they handle me?"

"I taught them everything I know. And don't you think I handle Rita pretty well?"

"Ok Chad, you know how I like to bring order quickly, we'll go with your plan. You set-up shop in NY for a couple of months and we'll have your starry eyed protégés rock and roll here."

"Good morning, Ms. Rita, is everything ok?" Amanda always looked so chic and impeccable no matter what the hour of the day. She was so perfect for the Monet image. "Ms. Rita, it looked like you were in a real panic when you came. Is everything ok? I was finalizing reservations for Congressman Wade's Office. They booked a party of ten for next Saturday. "

"Amanda, how is it we have space for ten, with just one week's notice? You know how I feel about these politician using their power and influence to get something their constituents can't."

"Ms. Rita, I didn't do anything special on this, it was just divine intervention, I guess. We had space. Congressman Wade's office is always so gracious when we can't accommodate them. I always say, you can really separate the Christian from the heathen, when it comes to reservations."

"Ok but why are you so perky and grinning from ear to ear? Rita questioned Amanda with obvious impatience.

In her most polished Slavic accent, Amanda announced, "guess who's in Congressman Wade's party? Without waiting for a reply, Amanda blurted out "Reverend Owen Blake. You guys probably don't watch Christian programming but Pastor Blake has a mega ministry but more importantly, his ministry led me and my family to God." Amanda's pronouncement had more gravity than she knew.

Rita's whole demeanor changed, as if cold water was dashed in her face.

"Ms. Rita is something wrong? Did I say something? I know we avoid any mention of religion around here but my faith and belief are important

3

in my life. Do you know Reverend Blake? I didn't think you would know him since he ...

Chad, backing into the kitchen, interrupted the conversation with the intention of bringing levity, "Rita, let me run off to make some unleavened bread or cross buns or something?"

Rita, turned her head but not her mind, toward Chad.."Ok Chad, please don't say anything more about the matter we discussed earlier.."

Then Rita, being very mindful of her response to Amanda, turned to face her squarely... "So Amanda, you think I am a heathen and wouldn't know about this mega ministry.."

"Not at all Ms. Rita, I believe you know. I just don't talk much about these things because, you know, everyone here becomes so uncomfortable when you mention anything about God and faith or your religion. But Rita, I am a believer in Jesus Christ, I am born...

Rita finished Amanda's sentence. "Born Again/Saved/ filled with the Holy Spirit"?

Amanda looked astonished, yet satisfied that a piece of the puzzle now fit, "Rita, I felt you knew or understood because there was something that drew me to you."

"Amanda, I know more than you think". Ok so your "spiritual father" Reverend Blake, is coming to town" and you get to met him over lunch.

"Rita, I am so excited about meeting him. His ministry had such an impact on my life and my family's back home in the Ukraine. His ministry supports the pastor who runs the local church where they attend. Image, my mother, sister and bothers, were lost spiritually. But when I prayed for someone to introduce them to Jesus, a pastor came and he was sent from Reverend Blake's ministry. It is amazing how pieces came together. I'm sorry, I didn't mean to preach. The reason I came in, is to ask to do part of the customer service assessments on Saturday. I know that's your baby but I'd really like to come in to work as well as meet the pastor."

"Amanda, my dear friend, you may be blessed beyond what you could ever ask or think. I might take the whole day off and let you run the show on Saturday."

· · · · ·

Rita felt she was holding her breath the whole time while talking to Amanda. Retreating back to her office, which was always a place of peace with everything in order, French provincial furnishings with soothing colors all around she dropped in her chair. And as if she were able to breath again, she softly spoke the name.... "B l a k e, Owen Blake ".

Owen Blake in Washington, it didn't seem to fit the Blake she knew. But as a powerful mega pastor, with an international ministry, it made sense he would come to the political power center, the Nation's Capitol. Rita marveled that it had not happened sooner. But why was he coming now? Rita had not seen any advertisements of a major Christian gathering. She always kept up with those things when she perused the Christian Magazine that would mysterious appear in her office monthly.

Strange, in over 10 years, their paths never crossed or came close to one another. But then Rita created a life that was far from Blake's world, making an encounter highly unlikely. Rita was aware of the daily reminders of the high price paid for that gulf created between their two worlds.

But next Saturday, their worlds threatened to collide. She had come too far to sacrifice it all over a lunch.

The phone ringing interrupted her thoughts.

"Francois, honey, I was just thinking about you. How is your day going?"

"Fine my sweet, I just called to tell you I love you."

"I love you too, how about us going down to Charlottesville, and checking out that horse that we care and feed and you never ride."

"Rita, I love the idea and for you to step away from the restaurant on a boom spring weekend, well I must be special. But darling, I have those art pieces coming in from London next Saturday". You know how hard I worked on that deal and I need to be here to bring closure to that." But can we do it maybe before the end of the month?"

"Yes, yes, of course. So will I see you early or late this evening?"

"My sweet, I think early, you sound like you are missing me already"
"Bye honey"

CHAPTER 2

WHOSE REPORT DO YOU BELIEVE?

Ten years earlier in New Orleans ...

It was a typical Sunday in New Orleans, everyone always tried to clean up on Sunday, even Sam the neighborhood wino tried to get himself together on Sunday. But there was a major buzz in the air, "the big one was coming".

A stunning woman stood behind the pulpit and spoke with such authority and loves ..."Church let us rejoice and be glad in it. Yes, the weathermen are predicting a major storm, they call it a category 5 hurricane, they even gave it a name, Katrina, but whose report are you going to believe? I believe the report of the Lord." You may say, Pastor Arrita, you have options, you have a husband and a car and you work for Big Al, who can make anything happen, just for the asking. But let me declare, Arrita is not looking to her husband or Big Al. She is looking unto Jesus the author and finisher of her faith."

The congregation responds was resounding at it always was when Pastor Arrita minister to them with such power and conviction ...Amen sister. Amen sister. He husband, the co-pastor of their modest congregation always told her she was clear evidence that Apostle Paul was not forbidding all women from preach.

" As your pastor, I am not telling you to ignore the news or do foolish things; what I am saying is to put your faith in gear. Speak the Word. Our heavenly Father says in the 91st Psalm. We (you, me) that dwelled in the secret place of the most high shall abide under shadow of the almighty…"

· · · · ·

Rita shuttered as she reflected on those memories that had not been thought of in long time. It was easy to forget certain things when you don't have reminders around you. Church was her life back then but there was nothing of that life in her current world. Everything around her represented the world's definition of success. She lived a prominent and enviable life in a powerful town. It was far from the life of Arrita in New Orleans! However, the small bible that was once her mother's, kept in her beautiful desk drawer, always seem to call out to her whenever she opened that drawer.

"Rita"

Startled by the interruption. "Yes Amanda, come in".

"Rita, I just talked to Todd, and if you are not coming in next Saturday, do you mind if the two of us split the day? After, I greet the Congressman's party and meet Pastor Blake of course, and do the assessments. I need to leave. I am directing the children's chore that Sunday and we need practice a lot on Saturday.

"Amanda, I didn't know you were musically inclined and a chore director. But then I knew you were special."

You're special too my lady, I just wish you would share more of yourself. I know you have so much to give beyond what you do here at the restaurant. That's why hold on to your every word. They call me Rita Jr. and I take that as a compliment".

"Amanda, I am going to shock you again by quoting a passage of scripture that you should know very well, "forgetting those things that are behind and reaching forward to those things that are ahead" Philippians 3:13 if memory serves me correct."

"You're correct. You pulled that out like a regular theologian." Ms. Rita, you are a river that runs deep."

CHAPTER 3

SAFETY FROM THE FLOOD

Flashback to New Orleans

Standing in front of the bathroom mirror of their modest three-bedroom home, Rita applied makeup she rarely used except when going to work at the restaurant.

Rita was a good-looking woman; some described her as stunning. She was not pretty by New Orleans' definition of a pretty woman of color. She was well sculptured. She had perfect cocoa brown skin, but too dark for classic beauty in NO, her body was firm but not thin. Her lips were full and she had a very attractive gap in her front teeth, which she always hated. She voids to fix her teeth once her kids' teeth were taken care of. Her hair was thick and naturally curly. Another thing she wanted to fix once she could find a true hair stylist and their budget could accommodate the full salon treatment. Rita was different and possessed special qualities. She was always the one picked to lead something. However, she was ys shy by nature and enjoyed anything that allowed her to be alone with her thoughts.

As she applied her make-up, looking into her reflection, she rehearsed what she needed to say to her husband. When her husband suddenly appeared in the bathroom, Arrita launched into her script, "Honey, I think you and the kids should leave."

"O thou of little faith, what about your message on Sunday ... who's report will you believe"?.

"I know honey, but I'm thinking about all those unbelievers who are stirring up so much confusion and wickedness". The girls may not understand it all but they are hearing crazy things on TV and unsettling conversations out there. I just don't want them affected by all this."

"And, what about you... Pastor Arrita?"

"I told you, Al has a block of rooms reserved for the staff. He wants to be in a position to cash in on the panic even if the big one doesn't come. That's one thing about Al, he's a shroud businessman."

"Al, who is Al? Owen Blake we obviously annoyed by his wife's view of her boss. "He is not God! I am at a place Arrita, where I'm ready for you to tell Al and that restaurant Good Bye" Rita knew where the conversation was heading; where it always went. The only way she knew how to respond was to fight back with words that were intended to hurt. If she said nothing she would feel bad about herself and her life in general. So Arrita struck back, "And Reverend Blake, are you ready to tell the money that Al and that restaurant brings into this family, good bye. Why do we always get into a tussle around this subject ? You of all people should view my income as a blessing. It makes up for those non-tithing, disobedient members we preach to every week."

"Arrita, I trust God and God only and I know this family and God's church will make it without...Al."

Recognizing the pathway of the conversation, and it ultimate ending, Rita let her husband have the last word, at least aloud.

CHAPTER 4

HOUSE OF CARDS

Present Day in Atlanta...

"Lacy, Lacy", yelling at the top of his lungs, Blake then remembered the intercom. He had them installed in all the rooms to cut down on the yelling and to keep up with everyone in their expansive living quarters. He smiled thinking of the expression, you can take the country boy out of the country but you can't take the country out of the boy."

Activating the system, Blake used his smooth silky voice to beckon his wife, Lacy. "Lacy dear did you...."

"Hey, Reverend, I'm here" as she suddenly appeared in the doorway looking beautifully pregnant.

"And yes dear, I did find the French cuff shirts and I even bought some of those collarless shirts you like."

"Really, they are so hard to find, you must have prayed those in".

Lacy had not traveled much, so she had the luggage out and was packing a few items everyday to make sure nothing was left out. As she placed the shirts in the suitcase, with her back to her husband, softly she started the conversation she'd rehearsed for several days.

"Darling, I was just thinking, you know this may be the last time you and the girls are all together before they go off in their separate directions. Esther's going to Law school in Washington, D.C. and DeBora is going to be a freshman in college in the fall. I think you should redeem the time with them. I know they will always be your little girls but they are young ladies. Before you know it, they will have careers and become wives and mothers. I don't want you to miss this time with them. It won't come around again."

"Lacy, our family includes you and our babies and the girls." The girls would look at me like I had lost my mind, if I said you weren't coming on this trip." And Reverend Fauntroy would expel me from the ministry if I came to Washington, without you."

. . . . .

Every mall in Atlanta was always crowded, you wonder if people in Atlanta did anything other than shop.

Esther and DeBora were in that number.

Esther, the oldest of Owen Blake's two daughter, was methodical. She always wanted everything well organized and meticulously planned. Her father, Reverend Blake, always said her gift was in administration. Her interest in law was no surprise. But he believed she was ultimately called to the ministry, like her mother. He'd say God was just training Esther by way of Law School, like Moses in Pharaohs household.

DeBora, looked so much like her mother. Sometimes her father would shut his eyes to avoid looking at his young daughter too long. When he did glare too long, memories would flood his consciousness. DeBora was strong, mentally and physically. It was a shock at first to hear of DeBora's interest in attending college in New Orleans. However when Blake prayed about it, he knew God was in the plan.

Esther was uncomfortable with the mall scene so she impatiently beckon her sister "Deb, I need your help. I must find an outfit for our trip. I want it to make me look absolutely gorgeous so Washington will take note I've arrived. So DeBora, please stop people watching and help me find this perfect outfit!"

"Sis, the translation on that is, you want something to make Dexter boy, think about sinning and the operative word is, think?"

"Deb, honestly your crudeness sometimes is enough to get you put out of the church.

But in truth, all I want is for God to bring him to his knees and then for the outfit to cause his lips to drop a little and his eyes bulge just a little and only temporarily."

" Esther, I must say, you certainly are mindful of your words. Because it would be hard to love a guy whose lips drop and eyes bulged permanently.

But honestly Sis, I'm really excited about our trip to Washington. Knowing Grandma Alice lived there and mother went to school there. Just think some of the same streets we'll visit, they walked those very same streets."

"It's funny Deb, I almost forgot about that. Mom went to the same school I'm attending even though it was only for a couple of years as an undergraduate, before she married Dad. I also can't remember her face, mother's face. Dad made sure everything that reminded him of her was taken away.

Wow, there is so much we don't know about our mother and it really hurts sometimes.

I don't think dad or anyone ever understood our mother. Dad never understood why she was not with us when the floods came. He didn't understand mother's relationship with her mother, Grandma. I know Grandma went to live with her sister, after mommy quit college and married dad. But didn't they all stay together"?

"You know sis, sometimes I get kind of sad thinking about mom and her family and not knowing more about them."

"Well don't feel bad Deb, I don't think mommy knew much about her family or herself for that matter."

"What do you mean Sis?" But DeBora knew further inquisition was of no avail.

"No matter, Dab we need to get going, you know how I feel about malls".

"YahYah malls are for people who don't know their purpose. But maybe my purpose is to be a mall shopper?"

CHAPTER 5

THE GOOD LIFE

Rita's new black Cadillac was a change in car type but not in color for her. Rita always considered black the only color option for luxury cars. She owned black BMWs, black Mercedes; black Audis and now a black Cadillac. All owned in the past ten years. She could remember when a white Toyota Camry was her luxury car.

Her raised consciousness of American made products was a small personal statement of support for keeping the American car industry strong. In Washington symbolism was sometimes more important than tangible outcomes.

As she drove up her English Tudor home overlooking Georgetown University's campus and the river, Francois pulls up immediately behind in his gray Bentley. Strange enough, Black Bentleys were the only luxury cars, in her opinion, that did not look good in black. Besides, Francois didn't like black anything except for his woman.

Francois jumped out and met Rita at her car door and opened it. That gentile gesture was his trademark for the many years they had been together. Opening the car door. It was interesting, that her husband did the same thing. Many women complained that men would look at them like, what's wrong with you, is your arm broken before they would open the car door.

Singing my Sherrie Amor... as he approached and opened the door he started speaking to her in rapid French.

Rita, tried to answer in French but she finally waved her hands in defeat. "Honey, I told you not to talk so fast if you want me to get it."

"My sweet, I'm immersing you in the language. I told you the next time we go to my country, you are on your own with the language. Look at me, I'm on my own in your country."

"Well, I will just interact with French "southerners". Where they speak slow and easy."

They entered the house together, with peace and comfort greeting them. It reinforced the gracious, elegant soft and soothing abode they shared.

Their Spanish housekeeper, Teresa, greeted them in Spanish at the door.

Asking them in Spanish, what time they wanted dinner served.

Rita was always amazed that as a young child, she said she wanted to be a citizen of the world. She hated the black/ white distinctions in America and the USA vs. Foreign mentality. And now she was playing out that whole citizen of the world concept in her own life …. a French mate, a Spanish housekeeper, a Ukrainian assistant. It was evidence of the power of vision and words. The powerful world had capitalized on that reality but the people that know the source of that truth, still were not applying that nugget.. It was a thought Rita reflected on in fleeting moments.

Rita responded in Spanish, go home early tonight, I'll take care of dinner.

Muches gracious senior, reverting to English Teresa explained "I need to go home early, because we are taking our English teacher out for dinner."

"Are you bribing the teacher for your final grade?"

"Oh No, Seniora, we love him so much and he is such a kind man. He is a writer but he gives us time at the technical college to help us."

"Well enjoy, your dinner. I won't ask if you are taking him to the "Monet"

"It would be nice but some of my classmates would spend their entire month's pay there."

"Well, I need to think of ways for Monet's to be experienced by everyone.

Turning her attention to the sounds coming from the deck

"Francois, what are you doing out there?"

I'm making a fruit drink that one of the staff prepared for us today. It was wonderful so I wanted to try to make it at home. I know I 'am missing some ingredience but I believe the main parts are here.

Why don't you go up and change and come back and relax"?

There was a quality, Rita loved about Francois, and he always wanted her to enjoy the flowers. He wanted people in general to enjoy the flowers. He wanted you to enjoy the beauty of the world i.e., art, good food, good relationships. There was balance about him. He was very productive and results oriented, yet he always took time to enjoy the moments. Even when things appeared absolutely chaotic, he always managed to see something of beauty or of humor in the situation. Rita felt God, had His hand in their meeting because humor and beauty were things Rita seemed to have missed in her life. She knew God was not in support of the relationship she had with this wonderful man but she knew he was meant to be a part of her life.

Francois in the hot tub, responded to Rita's reappearance

"… My sweet, I've been waiting with fruit drink in hand. How's that for service."

"I put on shorts not a bathing suit. Why didn't you tell me the attire for the evening."

Well the great thing about being home is having an array of dress options. You can keep it on or take it off ….

. . . . .

"Church, the Resurrection was not just about Jesus getting up from the grave and now seated at the right hand of the Father."

This was a message Reverend Owen Blake lived and breathed, so it was no wonder the anointing and Holy Spirit was with him. He also knew it was on the hearers as well.

Reverend Blake continued, "No if Jesus was the only one to experience the resurrection then or religion would be without power or authority. But because Jesus, was resurrected, we are partakers of the power of that same resurrection. We were dead but now we are alive in Christ Jesus.

A chorus of amen thundered back at Reverend Owens.

Since starting his biweekly broadcast, he has contemplated having at least one broadcast with just he in the studio, talking to viewers. But he was the kind of preacher that needed feedback from those he shared the Gospel.

· · · · ·

Amanda was getting a live Stream of Reverend Blake's 7:30 a.m. message as she prepares for church service. Fortunately, the children's chore only sang the first and third Sunday, so she had a little more time at home during those off Sundays.

Rita, had run this particular path around Georgetown's campus for several months and the Student Christian Center was at the end of her run. After this run, on this particular Sunday morning, she was drawn to venture into the building. As she stepped in, the live stream of Pastor Owen Blake's Sunday message was coming across the flat screen hanging front and center in the lounge area of the facility.

"…the Resurrection was not just about.…

· · · · ·

Sunday's for Rita, always made her feels a little melancholy. It invokes memories of the days when Sunday meant church, church and more church all day.

But when she ministered something always happened. She would struggle preparing her messages but when she rose to preach the word, God would use her like a pencil to write the message on people's hearts. Her husband always told her he loved her preaching. He would say if she spend most of her time praying and reading the scriptures and less time on preparing her message, she would be one of the greatest preachers, man or woman of her time. That was always too much for Rita to take in so she continued to do what she knew to do.

Rainy Sundays made Rita's melancholy even heavier and Francois always knew the mood and made a special effort to get her out of it.

That afternoon as she sat, at the window box looking out at their English garden, Francois came in the room baring a gift. It was wrapped in plain brown wrapping and it had a simple square shape, like a book or picture frame. They agreed years ago not to give each other expensive gifts. The agreement was reached when they saw how they were getting into the mode of trying to outdo one another with their gifts. On no special occasions, they would give token gifts. Just to say I love you. Rita's last token gift was a jar of green pepper jelly (homemade).

Francois had a smile that made the whole world smile and he had it turned on as he approached her with his package.

Well, open it my sweet. Rita unwrapped the gift with hesitation, then as she saw, the frame and the painting inside, she could not hold back the tears. It was an original Monet painting. She had Monet copies and original prints all over their home and in her restaurants but never an original.

Authentic, Authenticity that was a word that resonated in her being. She wanted everything around her to represent that state of being....."authentic" Yet her very life was so far from authentic.

Francois, I don't know what to say. Yes, I do but it makes what I have to say even more difficult.

Rita, I love you so whatever it is, I'll still love you so what are you going to do about?

Several hours later, Francois looked washed and rung out. Rita was looking up at Francois lying on her back on the floor as though the foundation of the floor was the only thing that kept her from being swallowed up into the earth.

Francois finally responded, "Rita, I don't know what to say ...know forgive me my sweet, I do know, I love Rita. And thank you for explaining away those many times you'd withdraw from me and I'd feel at a lost.. Now I understand.

But more importantly, what about you Rita, What about you?"

Rita was literally counting down the days and hours before, Owen Blake would enter her world. It was Friday afternoon, in less than 24 hours Blake would be dining in her restaurant.

Amanda ..was looking over the reservations for Saturday when she asked..."Rita, when are you and Francois leaving on Saturday?"

" Oh Amanda, I'm sorry I didn't tell you, we will be in town.

Amanda, looking puzzled ..."so are you coming in tomorrow to do your "customer service check"

"No, Amanda, I might be in but I won't be on duty. This will be your and Todd's show tomorrow."

"So what are you doing this evening"? Amanda inquired.

"Francois is working late tonight and he'll be at the gallery at the crack of dawn tomorrow, so I thought I'd treat myself to dinner and a movie tonight."

Shall be seat you Madame at our finest table?

Well actually, I thought, I'd go to that new Chinese restaurant I've heard so much about, then on to the foreign film festival on Campus. It really pays off to donate to the fine arts department at the University, free access to these movie festival is really quite nice.

As Rita droves toward campus her radio was broadcasting an unfamiliar announcer's voice, then she remembers the car wash people did it again, they changed the station. She was drowned to what was coming from her radio …"I 'don't normally play this type of music on my program, but a friend of my is going through the valley of the shadow of death …so this goes out to her …. (Music Playing)

· · · · ·

Owen Blakes was always the last to board a plane. He used his time at the airport to do what he was born to do, minister to people. Having his entire family join him on the trip to Washington was something entirely different. His assistant suggested that he book an earlier flight but Owen Blakes don't want to leave Atlanta in mid-afternoon it would feel like an entire day was wasted traveling. He also liked the idea of landing in Washington in the evening. He remembered his mother-in-law talking about landing in Washington, going by the monuments and over the Potomac River. She use to say that passengers always made a point of looking out the windows when landing at Ronald Reagan National Airport in Washington D.C.

Jason, was Blake's assistant when he was traveling but he was like a son as well. Jason had adopted the Blake family as his own as well. His parents were still challenged and angry over the fact he was using his MBA from UVA to be a pastor's assistant. However, they didn't know how Pastor Owens's ministry saved his life when he was at a point of giving it all up.

Jason, Jason ....Pastor Blake would call his name twice when he was excited about something or wanted him to do something. "Give this young lady a book and CD from our last conference."

" I believe it will bless you young lady."

"Lacy, girls are we all together?"

DeBora being the outspoken one blurted out.

"Dad we have been ready, we've been waiting on you".

"Ok then let's go,

Lacy you ok?"

Lacy, always with a calm and quiet spirit assured him that she and the girls were fine.

As they boarded the plane, several passengers recognized Pastor Blake and he greeting them all in his typical warm and loving fashion.

Blake don't know why but something was stirring in him about the trip and so he settle in his seat and starting reading the book that always gave him comfort – his Bible.

· · · · ·

"Dexter, you got a haircut!" Reverend Fauntroy was a very conservative, disciplined minister and he ran his household in that same fashion. His son however, had reached a stage where he was challenging his father on many issues, the least of which was his person appearance. It was interesting that Dexter was challenging his father at this point when up to now he had pretty much done as his father wanted.

"Sir, I thought I'd clean up a little."

"Well we are going to have to get Esther to come up here more often so we can get our son to get a haircut." What do you think Mrs. Fauntroy?

Dexter looking rather sheepish after the comment, reminded his father that Esther would be moving to Washington to attend Georgetown Law School in the Fall.

"Dad, Esther is a very find woman that I would like to commit to in the near future."

"Dexter, let's talk about that later, right now I would like to look at my well groomed son and maybe hang out with him since my better half is holding a ministry meet this evening."

"Dad, don't put me off like that."

"We will talk son, we will."

"But Dexter, you must think your parents are deaf, blind and a little touched.

When we were in Atlanta last summer, we thought you were going to announce your desire to attend Morehouse Medical School but when you said you wanted to attend Howard we suspected that Esther was somewhere in the picture."

"Dad, you know that Howard has a great Medical School and it will allow me to assist you with some of those medical clinics you want the Church to support."

"Dexter, I am grateful to you and to Esther for thinking of me and the church in your planning. "

Reverend Fauntroy was always so serious so when he was in a joking mood, the entire atmosphere lightened up.

Dexter, wanted his mother to experience more of that light hearted nature from his father. She needed to be light hearted herself and have more humor and fun in her life. Dexter's mother was a wonderful woman but she was so overshadowed by his husband. That seemed to be common among powerful ministers and their wives.

· · · · ·

The movie Rita saw at the foreign film festival wasn't particularly good but it served its purpose, it was sad and it allowed Rita to settle into a comfortable melancholy mood. After all, she had a right to feel that way. In less than 24 hours here, her life could change forever.

She was so engrossed in thought before she realized she had walked to the Christian Student Center. She remembered the little café they had and decided to go in.

As she stepped in there was a group of students sitting on the floor and on the sofa and chairs listening to someone up front reading " If I parish I parish, Esther 4:14.

It was obviously a bible study group and the teacher went on to talk about Esther in the Bible ...

"Esther had an encounter with the living God. She decide she would not fear and would go forth boldly into the King's chambers"...

those words echoed back to Rita..Go forth boldly into the King's chambers.

Rita looked at the group leader and the leader looked back at her as though those words were spoken directly to her.

· · · · ·

Saturday, mornings were always peaceful and calm in Rita and François' home. Rita made sure of that because activity and chaos was the order of the day when she was a child and when she got married. Francios was definitely God send because he also was a seeker and protector of peace and calmness. When Rita first met Francios, she was sitting on a bench in the art gallery, meditating and totally engrossing herself in a Monet painting. Francois was so taken by her spirit and love of beauty.

Francois always aroused her so sweetly from a night's sleep.

She could hear his voice penetrating her consciousness

"Good morning my sweet" how are you"

Good morning, doing super fantastic thank you

" I like that answer"

"So what are your plans for today"

" I don't know but God know"

Francois had not heard Rita respond in that fashion but he knew she would be strong. What he didn't know was how they would come out of it. He loved his life with Rita. He didn't realize how much until, this threatening cloud appeared.He quietly kissed Rita on the forehead.

Rita, I will see later, all right? Do think you want to come over to the gallery today. I'll be busy but never too busy for you.

"Honey, I will be find and no I will not get in the way of you and your new art pieces. I love you Francois, I really do.

"Thanks my sweet, I really, really needed that.

CHAPTER 6

AND THE FLOODS CAME

Flashback to New Orleans

A helicopter line and hook came down to the roof top to lift them to safety. Rita could not believe this was happening, the streets of New Orleans were flooded. They were without electricity or water. Big Al could not take care of this one. Rita had never seen Al scared but she was seeing it now and she was doubly frighten. Where were her children, where was her husband, were they dead, was she going to die. So many things were flooding her mind as she saw the streets of New Orleans flooding.

Rita's life did not flash before her like she had heard would happen when death seemed near, rather the things she regretted appeared before her like a movie scene was let down before her eyes. She regretted not finishing her degree in Art History and not accepting the scholarship in Boston, not staying in Washington to be with her mother, not going to Paris on that one year student exchange program. Her life filled with regrets was laid out before her eyes. As she dangled through the air, being rescued from a city underwater and under seage her life seemed meaningless and pointless. When she was finally seated in the helicopter, she steadied herself enough to hear the pilot talking to the copilot.

"We are going to drop these folks at that bridge crossing just ahead. There is a bus that is suppose to pick them up from there. "

Panic and confusion was in the air and on the faces of men, women and children on the bridge. Rita, walk along the bridge in a fog. She wanted to feel something but there was no feeling anywhere.

"Lady, Lady, are you trying the get on the next bus going to Houston, Lady do you hear me?"

There was a young man moving his lips and words were coming out but Rita's mind could not process anything that was being said.

"Follow me" he said but physically guided he to the area he was taking her.

Rita, did not know she could speak audible until she heard herself say ..."yes, I'll follow you".

There was no space or time ....

Rita's senses were aroused with the smell of the bus fumes and body odor. The person next to her was snoring and seemly comfortable on this bus ride to (where)

" Excuse me, excuse me, I'm sorry to wake you but I am really confused what is going on, where am I."

"God Lady, I am really glad to see that you're alright"

"What do you mean alright" responding as she withdraws toward the bus window.

"First, my name is Randy Moore, I' ve been sort of your body guard for the last 24hrs.

"You were kind of wondering around like you where in a daze or out of it, which is understandable. There was just too much going on for a lady like you to be left alone. So I just attached myself to you".

"How did I get on this bus and where are we going."

"We are going to Houston and you walked on this bus, and you don't remember any of it do you?"

"The only thing I remembered was dangling in the air from a helicopter" I guess I'll always remember that. Rita wanted to remember more but she could not get beyond being rescued by a helicopter from a city underwater".

"By the way what is your name"?

"My name is ...Rita" Thank God I remembered my name. Where we going for God sake".

"We are going to Houston it seems like NO can't accommodate all us homeless folks so they're busing us to Houston for shelter. By the way I told the Red Cross you were my wife. I thought things would go better for us if we were a couple"

"And does your wife have a name"? I told them your name was Regina. That was my grandmother's name".

"So what happens when we get to Houston"?

"Your guess is as good as mine"

"So who are you Ms. Rita, are you married? Do have kids, what did you do in NO, where did you live, what do you do; so what where you doing the day NO flooded?

"Wait wait one question at a time."

"Yes, I am married and have two beautiful little girls." We live on Borderstreet. and I worked at the Maximillion restaurant and the staff was staying at the Claremont bed and breakfast near the restaurant. Oh and by the way I am a preacher by calling."

"Wow you just said a mouthful. No wonder, I was on assignment to guard you."

"ya like angel on assignment"

"So where do you think your family is now?"

"I don't know but once I get to wherever we are going, I will find out"

" I know they are not dead" God would have told me if that were so"

"what about you" your family?

"I was visiting your fair city from London". I 'm a writer. "

"So how did you get catch up in all this mess, If I were you I would have taken the first plane back to London."

I told you I'm a writer, and interesting enough, I was having writer's cramps and that's why I knew I needed to step away from London." Something happened in NO that would define a moment in history, so I knew I was in the right place at the right time. Besides, I now know I was assigned to take care of you.

Well, I thank you Randy, I will be forever grateful. But seriously, this is a nightmare and I would think you'd want to wake up from it very soon.

Fortunately, I will get past this, but unfortunately many of the people on this bus will be living this nightmare for years to come."

The bus driver pulled into a rest area and announced that the passengers could get off for a half hour but if they were not back promptly, they would be left.

Rita wanted to tell the driver, in case he didn't know it, he was transporting wounded soldiers, and wounded soldiers should never be left behind. But Rita knew she was not thinking clearly, so communications on her part were best limited.

Rita, marveled that she knew no on the bus or at the rest area where other NO buses had stopped. She knew no one which was odd because she knew many people in NO because of preaching and through the restaurant. It was as though she were in another country. People were amazingly quiet at the rest area. Everyone seemed in shock. Randy really took his assignment seriously, by following Rita around up to the point of standing outside the restroom waiting for her to emerge.

"Randy, I think you can take a break from your assignment of guarding me, I'll be ok besides I need to walk and pray a little while we are here."

Randy wanted to cling to Rita more for his sake than for hers. As he walked back to the bus, he realized the last 24hrs were free of depress and thoughts of suicide. He felt alive and engaged in life again. There was so much to write about, so much to describe, the question was, where he should start.

Rita, returned to the bus knowing that something had happened to her. Her life back home, the kids, her husband, her church, it all seemed so far away and unattainable. She was sad and quiet when she sat down in her seat. Randy was already in his seat and busy writing in a notebook he must have acquired at the rest area.

"I didn't see a store around" where did you pick up those items," pointing toward the note book and the pen.

"I sweet talked the attendant and got her to get these from their office.

I told her I was writer and I would mention her in the next piece I wrote."

"And what will be the next piece? I thought I'd write about you."
"Then there won't be much material."
"But I have a feeling there is more material than one book can hold."
Rita, shrugged and turned toward the bus window wanting to be alone with the many thoughts flooding her consciencousness.

· · · · ·

Mrs. Moore, your husband said he was heading back to NO to check on your property but I need a few more pieces of information for the data base. The red cross is trying to keep families connected. So besides your husband are there any other members of your family?

Rita was silent for what seem to be an eternity, long enough to reflect on the rescue on the regrets that flashed be for her, the life she lived before the flood.

Mrs. Moore did you hear me, are there any other members of your family living in NO?

"No." The response echoed back into Rita's ears and it sounded loud enough for the entire facility to hear.

"No, there is no one but me and my husband."

"So do you want to be put into the data base system since your husband already knows where you are?"

"No, I don't think that will be necessary."

"Can I look for friends or neighbors in the data base.

"Yes, we want people to reconnected. Are there some names you have in mind? "

"Yes. Blake, Owen Blake,"

"Just a moment, let's see what comes up."

"No there is nothing in the system on that name. But remember we just started this so it may show up in a couple of day. So you need to keep checking the system. Also, this system only captures people who had to evacuate to shelters or are displaced from their homes. As you know, not everyone was impacted like that.

Yes, I know. Rita responded as she looked around and saw a sea of people that looked like her.

· · · · ·

CHAPTER 7

WORLD ON COLLISION COURSE

Amanda arrived earlier than usual that Saturday. Since she was taking Rita's place as the customer service assessor, she wanted go beyond what Rita would do. But Rita was a tough act to outshine. She was also excited about Reverend Blake dining in the restaurant that day. It was just a wonderful Saturday morning and she was excited about being alive and enjoying it all.

As time passed, the restaurant, became more and more alive. On Saturday and Sunday, the Monet opened early for bunch so by 10:30 a.m. customers were already entering the restaurant. The bunch customers were the usual crowd with standing reservations. They were the wives taking husbands out before their golf games, they were grandparents wanting to eyeball their grandchildren between breaks from school or the married couples not knowing when they will have their next meal together, or the singles that are tired of the dating pandemonium so that take solace in taking themselves out for bunch, and then there are the veteran legislators that want to get in and out before the freshmen and constituents show up. Now if those veterans need to do some politicking, the order is reversed. They are in at the peak of lunch and dinner hours.

Congressman Wade's reservation time was a combination of things, he wanted to show one of his most influential constituents, Reverend Blake, that he is a mover and shaker in Washington and show off the rich, powerful and beautiful of the south. He knew Blake would not let him down. Blake was a striking man and his wife was stunning. She seem to radiate even more as a pregnant woman. He also had a very tragic yet triumphant story. The passing of his first wife in the Katrina floods 10 years ago and his rise from a small town country preacher to a renown minister were storybook backdrops. His daughters, from his first marriage, were also lovely role models of bright, progress Christian young people with purpose. Blake would really, give him a run, if he ever turned his interest to politics. He had all the ingredience of a "poster politician". But politics was clearly far from Blake's interest. He was on a mission from God or ...

· · · · ·

Reverend Fauntroy, his wife and son Dexter, were the first to arrive at the restaurant. His wife had fussed all morning about her outfit. She seemed to have grown more insecure over the years. He was impatient with her when he detected that insecurity and his impatience seem to make matters worse. She always emerged looking impeccable but her internal state was far from orderly.

Dexter on the other hand was a striking young man. He had the world on his side and he acted as such. He finished his undergraduate work with honors, he was accepted in Howard University's Medical program and his future wife was coming to Washington to study law at Georgetown University. Life was perfect from his perspective.

Amanda, greeted them immediately when they entered the restaurant. She knew Reverend Fauntroy by sight because he had come to her church on a number of occasions.

"Reverend Fauntroy we are so glad you could be with us this afternoon at the Monet Gardens."

"Thank you we have been looking forward to it". "Am I the first to arrive?

Yes, you are and we can seat you and your family immediate. We have you in the gardens, our loveliest area of the restaurant. You can look out on the gardens. You won't mind the wait, if there is one, taking in the gardens and the fragrance.

Reverend Fauntroy's wife Elizabeth, was particularly taken by the garden view since she worked hard at theirs. Her eyes widen as she saw all the flowers in bloom and the landscape arrangements of every flower and plant in the garden. As they settled in at the table, Reverend Fauntroy's wife looked out over the gardens glowingly, then she turned her attention to the table with a tense, pensive expression. Reverend Fauntroy noticing his wife's mood change, and immediately snapped at her with his dictatorially speech pattern.

"And so what is bothering you now"?

"I'm not worried, I just think we should have picked up Reverend Blake and his family"

"I told you he was being brought by the hotel chauffeur service" and I might add a stretch one."

"God is good to his servants!"

I know you said that but it is would have been nice to chat before we came together with Congressman Wade?

Liz, there would have been seven people to fit in our car?

You, know Dexter would have volunteered to pick up Esther.

Well we are here and ….

Before he finished his sentence, the remaining members of their party appeared, being lead by Amanda.

· · · · ·

Parked across from the restaurant, Rita watched a limousine pull up and out came a very dashing figure… Owen Blake. Rita felt as though she was struggling for air and then emerged a loving woman that was obviously well along in her pregnancy and two young ladies jump out with such energy and excitement it could be seen by all who were around.

Rita's eyes filled with tears and her mouth trembled saying words she had not spoken in years … my children… my daughters.

· · · · ·

The party of 10 chatted as though there was so much ground to cover with very little time to do so. Dexter and Esther chatted as though they were the only ones at the table; the Ministers wives; Lacy Blake and Dorothy Fauntroy were engaged in a conversation about the women's conference being hosted at their church with hopes Lacy could fit it into her schedule.

Rev. Blake; Rev. Fauntroy and Congressman Wade were huddled and engaged in a cyclical debate of separation of church and state.

Reverend Blake, you know your influence in Atlanta with voters of the Christian faith, was instrumental in getting the 7th District back into the Democrat column.

Yes, but as you know I don't talk politics in my pulpit. I speak the Word of God and let people vote their conscience.

Bating the conversation, Congressman Fauntroy asked, Reverend, I have heard talk you might be interested in running for office if the opportunity presents itself?

Laughing lighthearted Blake responded, Whoever said that must be fellowshipping with the devil. I am a preacher, always have been and always will be. I would be stepping down, no disrespect intended, if I pursued anything other than God's call.

Reverend Fauntroy injecting himself in the conversation…Now gentlemen we came here to have a light and relaxing luncheon so let's get out of the political arena.

I agree, DeBora echoed, who had been observing her surroundings and making note of all the people she had seen on CNN regularly, seated in the restaurant. So Congressman Wade, will we be able to tour the capital or sit in on a full session of Congress. Well, my dear we have arrange a guided tour for you and your family but I'm afraid there won't be any sessions this week because we're on break. You guys have spring break too, I think I want to be a Congresswoman, I like the schedule. DeBora was enjoying the attention from the Congressman and was taking advantage of her father's atypical lose control of the conversation.

Amanda appears at the table with two waiters in toe and with looks that said ask and it shall be given unto you.

Let me again, welcome you to the Monet Gardens of Washington.

Is there another Monet Gardens, like of Atlanta DeBora asked.

Well not yet, but we have a very fine establishment in New York and we are hopeful we will one in Canada soon.

Let me say that my assistant had nothing but praises for this restaurant and for your service, Congressman Wade shared with their host.

No doubt we are having a customer service crisis in America, along with other crisis on the horizon but your service stands as a shining example of excellence in its finest.

Thank you Congressman Wade, our leader and owner of this restaurant believes in quality service and the entire staff strives to exhibit that in all we do here at the Monet.

Now if I may assist you in some menu recommendations and I might add, everything is outstanding. We do have so chef choices I'd like to point out to you.

. . . . .

Rita, knowing the exact area where Blake and the others were seated, move her car to see the party of 10. They were seated in the most scenic area of the restaurant.

Her eyes were fixed on her girls. A picture was truly worth a thousand words. Esther, was obviously very taken by the young man that was seated next to her. Their eyes and conversation never seem to divert from one another.

And DeBora, seemed so much like her grandmother, Rita's mother. She was the "eyes", always observing and taking in what most people overlook.

They were obviously very fine and respectful young ladies. Blake had done a good job, which is why she felt, in an attempt to relieve a tremendous pain, her decision was for the best. In some ways, she knew Blake nor she would have achieved what they have now, if she had said "yes" there were people in NO who would be looking for her. She remembered the scripture, a house divided cannot stand and the Blake household in NO was divided.

But now it was decision time, will she inject herself into the world she left over 10 years ago.

. . . . If I parish I parish.

. . . . .

Everything sounds wonderful, Lacy responded after hearing chef choices, but then again I'm eating for two so don't mind me.

Amanda taking the opportunity to speak to the guest in a personal way shared ....

May I also take the opportunity to say how honored I am to serve you. Pastor Blake I must share that it especially wonderful to meet you personally, because it was through your ministry, I accepted the Lord Jesus Christ into my Life. And it is your outreach mission in the Ukraine that is sharing the gospel with my family they are growing in the Word of God.

Praise God, Reverend Blake blurted out, did you hear that. That's what it's all about. Young Lady, I thank God for you. I know the ministry is reaching many people but when I hear personal testimonies like yours, I praise God for His faithfulness. Are you in a good church now? Yes Sir. Well if you were seeking one, I would recommend this man's church to you, patting Reverend Fauntroy as he spoke.

Now I know this table will be spread well since one of His servants is spreading it. God Bless... Amanda and I hope if you are ever in Atlanta, you'll visit us. But before you take off and do your customer duties that I know you do so well, I'd like us to pray with you. Lacy was always a little sensitive about how Blake would breaks out in prayer, even in "tongues", anywhere. But, she had grown to accept it even though it was it was sometimes a stretch, given her Catholic up bring.

Father we thank you for Amanda ask that you hasten to perform all the desires of her heart. Strengthen her, set her on the pathway you have ordained for her from the foundation of the earth. Let her be a bright light in this place, so that she may tell of your mercy, glory and grace. We thank you. In the precious name of Jesus. Amen.

Thank You Pastor Blake Thank You. I love my job here and the one thing I'd been praying about was to be more of a witness in this place.

As Amanda was backing out of the room. Rita appears at the entrance of the terrace and gently tapped Amanda.

Ms. Rita... you're here. Looking back at the guest seated at the table she grabbed Rita's hand to bring her into the room.

It is my pleasure to introduce you to our owner and visionary of the Monet, Ms. Rita Moore.

"Jesus, Jesus"

Reverend Blake are you ok, you sounded like you were ready for the rapture. Reverend Fauntroy responding to Blake's outburst in light humor.

Lacy was us to those outburst because they would happen anywhere and at any time. Owen would tell her since he walked and talked with God all day, there should be nothing unusual about called on the name of Jesus while talking.

Rita ignoring the outburst entered the room with her million dollar customer service greeting,

Good Afternoon everyone, it is my pleasure to have you here with us at the Monet, today. I know Amanda has been taking excellent care of you but if there is anything I can do for you this afternoon, please don't hesitate in letting me know.

· · · · ·

Flashback to NO

Motor boats, what an odd sound hearing them come to rescue you from your house that was flooded up to the ceiling. Owen Blake and his children were escaping from their flooded home by climbing on top of the roof. He saw the fear in the eyes of his girls but he knew he needed to be calm. He needed to reassure them all was well. Even though there house was flooded and they did not know whether their mother was ok.

Daddy where is mommy? Mommy is safe, you know she's at the restaurant so they have a safe place to stay until this is all over. Helicopters were hovering in the area but nothing was happening, he would stand and wave his arms in the air but it appeared as though the pilots were just observers rather than angels of rescue. Blake prayed like never before, he prayed for his girls, for his wife but his prayer for himself was not to be rescues or that his life be saved but that his life be Transformed. He realized he had been going through the motion of serving and being a servant of God but he had not really given his life totally to the master and creator of his life.

He didn't know what it all meant but those were the words screaming in his belly. "O Lord transform me; renew that right spirit within me".

Someone was calling from the water. It was an official in a boat, not knowing if they would also observer as the helicopters had been doing, Blake looked first. He then stood up and started yelling at the boat pilot.

"We need help, will you help us".

The pilot responded asking

"How many are there with you?";

"Three, me and my two little girls".

Pilot yelled back,

"Catch the rope and secure it to something stable on the roof."

Blake looked about for something stable on the roof and at the same time he realized he had never been on the roof.

Strange that he thought of the scripture about Peter on the roof top. Peter had a vision from the Lord; however he felt like he was having a nightmare on the roof.

· · · · ·

Blake was speechless, and struggled to breath as he looked upon this woman at the entrance of the room. She was someone he knew, yet she was not. This woman at the entrance was exquisite in elegance, beauty and grace. She was the picture of Washington power clothed in fine linen. Yet, this woman was someone who had once walked and talked with God and had a life that expressed that relationship. Her hands were clasped together in a position of prayer, she stood as though in a pulpit of authority, and she smiled and greeted as though she were sharing the love of God with the people before her. This was not Rita the owner of Monet, but Arrita, Owen Blake's wife, the mother of his children, a great pastor and a woman that had been declared dead.

Blake managed to gain composure and excuse himself to escape to the men's room.

Rita continued to greet the dining guest at the table, engaging in light banter with the younger members of the party. As she glared at her daughters, a flood of memories overwhelmed. My girls, now lovely young ladies. She'd missed so much but now a door stood before her opened albeit only cracked; she could not shut it again.

"Now if you will excuse me, please enjoy your stay and don't hesitate to let us know if you need anything"

Rita, backed away from the table with her eyes fixed on her daughter, as if wanting to take in every aspect of their being.

Once she had exited the room, she walked swiftly, restraining herself from running, to her office. She had to make herself breath because the air seemed so thin. Bursting into her office wanting to exhale, she found herself grasping as Blake sat at her desk with his eyes fixed on the doorway. Several moments passed before any words were exchanged and those moments felt like an eternity.

Blake spoke first, in that tone that after so many years, she still knew so very well. Arrita, no excuse me, it's Rita now isn't it?. Do you know what you have done? Do you know what you have done? Rita do you know.... Blake seemed to have trailed off in exhaustion.

Blake, please, don't you want to know what happened to me; don't you want to know my side of the story ; don't you have any feelings about me being alive; don't you have any feelings of joy that I'm alive?" Rita's voice trialed of being exhausted from her list of question.

"Please just stop Rita, this is not about you." Stop talking about what happened to you. Why not ask what happened to, our children, very young, innocent children, when they thought their mother was gone."

"Blake I know you don't understand but it would have been a terrible outcome for those girls growing up with a mother that was operating as a shell of herself. I was living but not really living."Those girls are strong now, self assured and confident, they would not have been so, had I stayed. But Blake I don't believe your true feelings are rooted in our girls, it's really about you ; your storied life of victory over defeat; and your international, mega, ministry. You have questions of your own; how will my resurrection affect your mega ministry. You aren't even thinking about your wife, who appears to be ready to bring new life into the world.

It's funny, it was the ministry then and it's the ministry now that drives your life."

"Rita, don't you stand there and use the ministry as an excuse for the horrible act you committed."

" Blake, don't you want to know what happened just out of simple compassion?"

" No!"

. . . . .

"Reverend Wade, I don't know what's happen to Owen, would you check on him?" Blake's wife was usually very calm with his disappearances because he never walked in a straight line. There were always people to encourage or witness to along the way. But something was unsettling Lacy and it was not the babies getting restless.

Reverend Fauntroy rose from his seat chuckling

"knowing Blake he is probably preaching to someone in the hallway."

· · · · ·

Rita sat at her desk, slumped and drained as though life had been ripped from her very being. Sobbing quieting Rita keep whispering

"God what can I do ..what can I do ...what can I do?"

Rita began to drift back to that dreadful day when she was rescued by helicopter, after the storm.

· · · · ·

The rescue copilot was shouting on the bullhorn ..."put the harness around your waist and we will do the rest. Please move quickly! Rita, could not believe the whole scene of what was happening, the city was underwater. The unthinkable was happening before her eyes. She could see others yelling for help but she was being lift up. When she was finally seated in the helicopter, it was like an outer body experience, watching things unfold. Then as though a sledge hammer came down on head she screamed ..."my children"! What had become of her children, she knew their father would take care of them whatever the situation.

However, thoughts of her husband were very detached. She wanted him safe but she did not want to be back with him in the way they were. Why where these thoughts coming up. She commanded her mind to Stop. Stop thinking.

The pilot was speaking to her but she could only see his lips moving

"Are you all right? He asked. I must go back to pick up other people, so I am going to land on the bridge. You'll be picked up by a bus that is taking you people out of the city."

Rita was not weak but she felt helpless sitting looking out from the helicopter. As the helicopter started to descend, she wanted to just jump out and be done with it. Where is your faith Rita, there was that soft voice she was familiar with, bubbling up inside her; I am your Father and I will never leave you.

CHAPTER 8

WITHOUT A CHOICE

Blake was moving without any since of time or space. He could not let his girls see fear or anxiety in his face. But his heart was racing. He could not reach his wife; his city was underwater; his faith was faltering. God what is happening? He screamed this in silence, as he took the girls to the safe place he and his wife had prearranged in case they could not get out of the city. How could this be happening? There were many questions going through his head, as he moved without express or sensation. Blake was not the pastor, or the spiritual leader at this point, he was a man who was lost and looking to find his way. "Pastor Blake; Pastor Blake."

The call of his name interrupted the thoughts that were flooding his mind.

"Pastor", " Hey Jesse are you alright? "Pastor we are trying to get the older people out of their homes but some of them refuse to go." Do you think you could do something Pastor". Jesse I would but I have to get the girls out safely and I don't know where my wife is right now. I understand pastor, but you know Rita is ok. She's uptown with Big Al right?

Pastor Blake remembered his last conversation with his wife about Big Al and it was not a good exchange.

Rita wandered the bridge looking for something to give her a sense of reality. There was nothing. Everyone was in a daze. Then a gentle hand touched the small of her back and a voice softly spoke into the ear.

"Let me help you to the area where the buses will be coming." Rita, was in a fog and could not quite process the statement about a "bus". What bus? Where is it taking me?

"I want to go home to my husband and my children." "I'm sure your family is safe but right now we need to get you to safety and you wondering around it not safe… so please let me help you."

His voice was the first soothing element Rita had encountered in the last eight hours. So she followed his lead obediently. They did not verbally communicate after that; everything seemed to be accomplished through eye and hand gestures and silent motions.

· · · · ·

The fumes from the bus was the first thing she noticed when her eyes opened. She soon realized she was also on a bus going somewhere. And beside her was a man who was quite striking with his hair braided and his diamond ear ring sparkling. This was not the sought of man she would ordinarily notice or find appealing but there something about this man that made Rita ponder. He then turned toward her and greeted her as though they had just awaken from a leisure slumber.

"You had a nice long sleep there." He spoke casually. I was wondering if you would sleep throughout the trip. You were obviously tired and weary."

Rita shot back feeling agitated and confused. "Where are we going and who are you?"

I'm sorry we did not do introductions but there wasn't any time for all the formalities". I'm Joshua Scott, I'm from Canada by way of London. I came to New Orleans or better still I was lead to NO, looking for a story but this was not exactly the story I intended to cover."

Rita was still trying to wrap her mind around all that was happening and still trying to take in the information this person sitting next to her was sharing. He was the person who could tell her where the bus was going. There was a strange feeling of both relief and heaviness. The heaviness was obvious but where was the relief coming from. "Where are we going?" She blurted.

"We are on the way to Houston? Have you ever been there?"

"No I have not".

"Well I'm sorry this is not exactly the best way to visit a city, for the first time."

Rita remembered how she wanted to go to Houston, for a conference but her husband was always saying they could not miss service or they could not afford to get away. Rita always had a desire to travel; to see different things; to meet interesting people to get away from the small minds and thinking of New Orleans.

"When will we get to Houston"?

"It normally takes a few hours but I think we are going to make a few stops before we get there".

A baby's cry was the first time Rita was aware of other passengers. Up until then, Rita had only been aware of her immediate surroundings; the window; the man that sat adjacent to her; the stains on her clothes and the body odors in the air.

But the baby's cry brought the reality of the flood back into her consciousness just as the waters came flooding into New Orleans. A bus load of people leaving the familiar and entering only God knows.

CHAPTER 9

ANGELS ON ASSIGNMENT

"This is our only rest stop before we get into Houston, do you want to get off? Rita was still moving in slow motion.

As she attempted to respond to her seating companion, she managed to put together a few coherent sentences "Do you know where we are? As if, it mattered. And Yes I think I will get out".

As she stepped down from the bus, it suddenly gripped her that she did not know what had become of her family. Had they perish, were they ok? But somehow, doubts of their safety were quickly dispensed with the knowing they were safe.

However, there was another thought, which was strange and frightening; there was a sense of freedom. Freedom from a life that was drowning her. It was amazing, she knew no one on the bus nor any of the individuals that were arriving from other buses. She continued to walk around in a daze with nothing to bring her back to some sense of gravity or reality. Joshua once again came to her rescue since she did not know which bus she was to return to. Joshua lead her back to the bus and back to their seats. She knew he had to be her angel because she was without any reservations in letting this stranger take control of her very being. Resettling in her seat she noted, her traveling companion scribbling ferociously in a notebook. She had not notice the writing prior to the bus stop and did not remembered any writing material at his disposal. Rita was beginning to feel the ability to access rational verbal communication she s inquired about his writing.

"Are you a writer"?

"How curious you would ask given the myriad of things I could be doing with this notebook."

"I asked because most people don't know how to use pen and paper anymore, if you can't text or twit or stream you haven't communicated."

"How right you are about our state of communications. It's a lost art of using those age old instruments. And the answer to your question is, Yes, I am a writing and I haven't been able to say that in a long while. So thank you for calling that out in me". I didn't know what I was for a while. I couldn't write but the more importantly, I couldn't feel anything to write." As he stared, pass Rita, out onto the landscape that whisked by on their ride to... Houston, he marveled how he had summed up six months of torment and pain into seven words ...I could not feel anything to write. It was six months ago that Joshua had lost his job as a journalist for the British World News. That job had defined him for over five years, his parents, his former classmates, and his former finance, referred to him as the foreign correspondent before they would speak his name. But in a blink of an eye or rather in the course of taking an ethical position on a story, the tides changed. He wasn't the foreign correspondent and it was as though he was no longer Joshua the person.

"Are you all right? You looked like you were in another world."

"You could say that I was, of sorts, in another world."

"It's strange, in this past 48 hours, you have attended to me, I 'm not use to being in that position, I'm the one usually attending to others. Rita was the pastor that everyone called upon. Asking you about how you are doing and being honestly interest is a familiar role and one I've accepted with a purpose."

"That sounds very magnanimous, Ms. Rita, but in my years of observing people, places and things, in high and low positions; with the rich and the poor; with the famous, and the ordinary, I've found a common denominator. Everyone wants to be seen, heard and valued in the purest sense of who they are."

"Well Mr.....?" Who is this person, I've been so vulnerable with, in the space of 48 hours. She had not thought of her children or her husband or the ministry or anyone she had left behind in NO. What was happening?

"The name is Joshua".

"How could I forget that name, Joshua lead the Israelites into the promise land. Well Mr. Joshua, I hear your world view on what people want but at this juncture, I feel like most of our plans didn't include this calamity. Want we want right is for the city, the state and our government to help us. They are suppose to be there if something goes wrong; but the city wanted people to be adults and take care of themselves; families wanted families to be there to rescue them, religious folks wanted God to work it all out. Yes, I hear you Mr. Joshua but if there is one thing I'm getting from all of this is, stop looking outside for your help. Your help is at hand."

"Well Ms. Rita, for a woman that seems to be totally oblivious to all that was happening around her, you certainly waxed clearer than any philosopher I have ever met. It even had a bit of a theological tone."

"Joshua I don't want to sound preachy, I know what that sounds like and it always turns authentic people off." I 'm just beginning to understand some things that have been bubbling within me for several months. I can't believe all those all those things swirling around in my spirit are reduced to seven words. "All you need or want is at hand."

"Yah, I also understand the power of seven words, more than you know." The remaining leg of the trip was passed with silence that was very loud. Rita and Joshua both pondered their seven words that would transform their lives forever.

Upon arriving in Houston, it was nothing short of chaos. They were dropped off at a civic center or an arena that looked like a refugee camp, if you were to depicted such a place. People were being herded like cattle and there was no space where people were not. Everywhere, there were cots, there were tables set up with different organizations represented and the media surrounded the place with camera, reporters and photographers. There was the red cross, FEMA, social security, the IRS, the postal service. In the short time being in this environment there was already a rumor mill and it was relaying that important people would be visiting this "refugee camp" within hours. That is why there was such a presence of state and federal organizations.

It was funny to Rita how everyone was there, the intent was to be helpful but no one seemed to realize they were dealing with war victims who really were not of sound mind to do any type of business. As Rita sat and waited for Joshua to return, a woman with a tablet approach her. She had a warm face and she smelled so fresh which was wonderful, given the aromas she had taken in from the bus. It was strange that in this state of displacement, she had found herself.

"Good Morning I am Sally Smith from the Red Cross, your husband sent me over because he said you were still a little weak from all you've been through these past couple of days."

Rita was trying to grasp all that was being said, my husband sent you? Is Blake here, why didn't he come? Where was Joshua? Given her confusion, Rita, thought it best to do more listening and so she gave Sally, leeway to state what she was there to do.

"You husband said he is going back to NO and he wants to get you out of this place, as soon as possible. I think I can help make this happen but I need a few pieces of information from you.

Now your husband said your name is Rita Moore and you are a businesswoman and you do not have any children."You husband's name is Joshua and he is a writer. You folk are very fortunate, if there is any fortune in this catastrophe. You folks don't have any children to look after or any elderly people you are caring for. It has been particularly hard on those two group."

Rita, felt as though the woman's words were being blasted over a loud speaker, "so you don't have any children and your husband's name is Joshua". Joshua, leading me to the promise land.

"Ms. Moore, is there anything that needs correcting or you need to add anything?"

This was the decisive moment, it all could go back to what was by simply saying My name is Rita Blake, my husband's name is Owen Blake, I have two little girls and I am a pastor.

It seemed as though a lot of time passed between the question and Rita's answer. Before she answered, Rita saw not her whole life pass before her but all her regrets and lost dreams. Not finishing her degree in Art History, not staying in Washington and not working for an art museum, not liking the way she looked, not having interesting friends and associates, not being financially independent and not having a marriage that made her better. All these things streamed before Rita and as she answered, it was like an outer body experience.

"Yes. Everything is correct. So what is next". Well Ms. Moore, you can get a voucher for temporary housing here in Houston, or if you have friends or relatives in another part of the country. We can get you funds to get to that other place."

"I would like to get to Washington, D.C."

"Do you have someone you can stay with ?"

"Yes, I am familiar with the area, I use to attend college there, Howard University."

"Well Ms. Moore, I'll see about getting you some transportation and are there people you need to check on? We have a data base that is far from complete but it may give you some leads on people you may be searching for."

"No it is just my husband and myself."

"Very well, I suggest you stay in this space, it is pretty horrific out there on the floor."

"thank you, you have been so kind."

"Well you husband was very familiar with our director, they apparently worked together, in Africa, so needlesstosay you are on our radar."

"So I am getting special treatment that is interesting, thanks for letting me know."

CHAPTER 10

BREAKING BREAD AND BREAKING SILENCE

"**B**lake, your wife sent me on a search and rescue mission. Where have you been man, setting up a satellite church in the restaurant?"

"No I was speaking with the owner about a birthday luncheon for Esther, she'll be deep in her studies when it rolls around, so I wanted to arrange something special for her on that day. Hopefully Dexter and a few of Esther's friends will help me out on this."

"You know Dexter, will be in on this before you ask. So let's get back to our lovely ladies."

Lacy's eyes were fixed on Blake when he returned to the table. No one else noticed but Lacy knew something was going on.

The lunch was winding up and it was like a wheel within a wheel at the table. Dexter and Esther were so absorb in one another they barely noticed anyone else; Blake, Wade and Fauntroy were deep in conversation regarding church and state and what is really behind the effort to make a hard demarcation between the two. The wives were discussing generational issues, women in ministry and children. DeBora seemed to be the odd one out but she was far from that since she was the facilitator of the conversations and interweaving the discussions between three groups.

"Dad, mom seem to think there is still some bias against women in the ministry, how can this be since some of the best preaching I have heard are women. So what do you say dad." Well DeBora, I agree women can be used mightily by God. However, women need to be covered in their ministries."

Now Blake, I don't think you should have many women in the pulpit. It is can split a church. I ordained several women and it was a mess. The husband of one was jealous of his wife's calling so he did everything to stress her out and in another case the husband started to be unfaithful with one of the congregates. I think the devil works overtime when women are called into the ministry. Now Blake when you were pastor in NO it was a model of having a woman in the pulpit. And I understand she was quit a firebrand.

But, now you have dear Lacy who is a true helpmate and Blake your ministry in Atlanta has exploded into an international platform. It has taken off into another dimension only God could orchestrate."

Pastor, I don't get wrapped up on this issue of women in the ministry, I just follow what I know is God's leading. Lacy has been a God send for me and the girls. I think without her we would be a shell of ourselves. We suffered more than anyone can know."

Oh dad, why do you want to bring up all that. We are here in Washington, dining at a wonderful restaurant, Congressman Wade is a fine host and all you fine people are just making me feel so marvelous."

"DeBora, you are such a dramatist, what will you do without me as your captive audience in all your drama."

"Esther, all I ask is for you to graduate and pass the bar so you can negotiate a lucrative contract for any movie deals that come along."

Last time I checked, entertainment law was not my area of focus.

Now girls, your future fame and fortune is very gratifying to Lacy and I, knowing we will be well taken care of in our twilight years but our hosts, I am sure, would like to bring this conversation back to the present."

"So Congressman, I look forward to visiting you at the Capitol this week."

" Blake, I am telling you the visit to the Capitol is worth the whole trip to Washington, aside from coming to my church of course.

As the Congressman's party appeared to be wrapping up their meal, Rita again entered their dining area. Everyone in the party was obviously enthusiastic about the whole experience. They readily shared their pleasure with Monet's owner.

Lacy once again sensed Blake's unease and irritation but she kept her peace.

The experience was worth the wait and I do thank you and all you staff for a wonderful afternoon. You have certainly helped me to impress my distinguish guests from Atlanta and my dear constituents here in Washington.

It was our pleasure and I hope we will see you again.

Amanda, my assistant, arranges many parties with notable figures but she was quite taken with this party and with you Rev. Blake.

Thank you and please let her know we will welcome her warmly whenever she comes to Atlanta.

CHAPTER 11

NO WAY OUT

The evening seem to come too slowly. The evening run on campus was like oxygen poured into Rita's lungs. Her mobile phone started to ring and she immediately thought it was Francois letting her know he was on his way home.

"Darling where are you, I hope you'll be home soon."

Rita this is Blake, you were obviously expecting someone else. Look, I don't know what to say to you this has been an earth shaking day. We need to talk and I don't have much time since my schedule is pretty tight. Can we meet back at your restaurant this evening after closing?"

"I am sure, I can be there by midnight, if I come at all. If I'm not there by then, I could not get away." What about your wife, how will you get away so late?

She knows, I take my prayer walks and sometimes it is hours before I return.

It was 10:30 p.m. before Francois car came into the driveway. The motor stopped but it was several minutes before the car door slammed and his footsteps where heard at the front door.

"Francios is that you? I am in the den."

Yes my sweet, I am on my way. When he appeared at the entrance of the room, he never looked so charming and warm. He was so gentle and warm and kind. He was always such a comfort and God knows, his gentle spirit was exactly what Rita needed during those years when shock and anxiety and fear enveloped her world. He knew her soul, he sense her love of art, and beauty from the first day they met. That first day they met, Rita was sitting on a bench in front of a Monet, painting. Francios was captivated by her total focus and commitment to the art piece. This gorgeous woman of color, commanded his soul and all that was within him.

Unlike American men, he waited no time in letting Rita know his interest. Rita was living in temporary quarters and it was obvious she was in a very unstable situation. Rita was gracious and very knowledgeable about art, so much so, it was a perfect fit to offer her a job at the museum as one their guides for the casual museum visitor. Most of the people on those tours knew little to nothing about art so you could call a Van Gough, a Monet and get away with it.

She was wonderful at the museum, she was more than wonderful, and she transformed the atmosphere. She had so many talents, she even turned the little café on the roof top of the museum into a very chic place to go at the end ones day at the museum. Francios saw her talents and he encourage her at every step. He did not hesitate in expressing his feelings toward Rita, after a year and a half of exclusive company at home and at work with Rita. She was still a mystery and it was apparent that deep waters ran within Rita but she made Francois feel alive and excited after so many years of just going through the motions.

They found a home together in Georgetown. It was near the museum but it was still secluded enough to feel like they had escaped the race going on around them. Rita was still doing wonders at the museum but there was so much more for Rita and Francois wanted to give her the platform to make it happen.

One evening, he planted the seed of Rita becoming a restaurateur, it was like she was waiting for instructions on what to do next. Francois came and game her not instructions but a blueprint.

Rita, by sweet, you are so gifted and I feel like a selfish man to keep your talents all to myself. I certainly don't want you to become my competitor in the art world but you have a wonderful flare for making people feel special. Your tours are the most requested at the museum and the café you transformed has become the place to go, even if you skip the museum.

I can't thank you enough, François, you have been so encouraging to me. It made me want to soar. I never had that in my life before. I think if you had been in my life earlier, there are some many things I would have accomplished. But I am so happy about fulfilling some of my dreams now.

Rita, I was talking to one of my clients this week and he was telling me about a property that would be a perfect place to open a restaurant in Georgetown. I told him I didn't think we needed another restaurant in the area but he was saying that there was still room for that old Washington dining and mystic. He specifically, mentioned you and how you have such a flare for entertaining and making places and things so special. He thinks the café is charming and that café on a grander scale, like a restaurant, would be perfect. You are as the host and owner could bring all the pieces together.

What do you think about that Rita? And, I was thinking about putting some of the museum pieces on display at the restaurant. It would be a great opportunity to introduce some of the cities', up and coming artists.

Francois, I don't know what to say. I am overwhelmed. I must admit, I am a little insecure about having what it takes to be successful. But I'm really excited you'll be in my corner. I don't know what to say.

Just say Yes.

I say Yes!

$\cdots\cdots$

I have been thinking about you all day. Did you see your daughters?

More than that, I showed up at their gathering. Blake, my husband, the girls,

They all saw me.

What happened? Did they know you? What did they say?

Blake knew me but no one else did. He wants to meet me this evening back at the restaurant. If you don't want me to go. I won't go.

Rita, I can't tell you not to go. I don't want you to but I don't think I can have all of you until you become one again. All of you has to reconnected.

You were resurrected this afternoon and I want your resurrection to be permanent.

Francois you are so good to me. You make me bold and strong. I love you for that and for your very being. You are an angel of light in my life.

Rita you don't have to tell me how much you love me, I know that but more importantly, I want you to know I am standing by you on any decision you make. I trust you. I trust us.

Well honey I need some quiet time before I go out this evening. What are you going to do while I'm gone?

I'll work on my book and work on the next show. Are going to be ok?

Yes. We will be more than ok. I hope when I get back, you will truly have the resurrected Rita.

CHAPTER 12

NO TURNING BACK

The Monet after hours always had a romantic atmosphere. The lights were soft, the flowers and plants throughout the restaurant stimulates all of your sense. There was such a wonderful and peaceful energy throughout the place, which Rita intentionally sought to establish and maintain. Many a night when Francois was working late at the museum, Rita would work at the Monet long after everyone had left. There were times when her knowledge of God's Word and the prayers that had gone forth, exhibited themselves strongly in those hours alone in that building. She would walk around every corner of the premise asking for God's forgiveness and thanking Him for his mercy.

As she sat in her office surveying all the things that brought her such pleasure, the sound of a car door closing and lights flashing in the office window signaled that the meeting was on. She knew that whatever happened it would transform her life forever. Rita went out the terrace door to greet Blake, who was dressed casually in a jogging suit. He wore shades and a cap on his head, as though he was truly engaged in a clandestine meeting.

"Blake you can come in over here. Is your driver going to stay?"

"Yes, I don't think this will take long."

Rita lead Blake back to her office without speaking a word. Blake was silent but several sighs reflected the meeting would be anything but a display of loving kindness. As soon as they entered the office, Blake stood unmoved after taking only a few steps inside the space. Rita headed for her desk, which was more of a barrier than a desk for conducting business. Blake stared and lower his head as if it was strenuous to maintain a straight up frontal glare.

Rita knew, even after all the years that had passed, not to start the conversation otherwise she would lose control immediately. She learned to be silent and bide her time. Wait him out. Don't be anxious. She had learned that not only from Blake but from life's lessons.

Rita, I am without words to say. What you have done is the height of deception, selfishness and Godlessness. Your actions impacted the lives of so many people and most importantly my children. Did the Word of God completely leave your consciousness, did God's call on your left tug at your heart, did the scriptures invade your thoughts, no one leaves to himself Arrita. You preach that scripture one Sunday and people came to give their lives to Christ hearing that word. But all of that seems to have abandoned you.

" Blake, those are our children and no I did not forget God's word, that's why I asked for his mercy and grace every day I was away." And He showed his mercy by allowing our children to grow into wonderful young women and allowing me to be who he fashioned me to be.

"No Rita, there are no "our children", as far as I am concerned you gave up your children 10 years ago. You have what you say God purposed for your life and it does not include those girls. You have no right, no interest and no claim to Esther or Debora. Thank God for his mercy and grace that they came through a dark storm and came out healthy, strong and loving girls. They could have gone another path but they were spared." Just as I was spared.

Maybe prayers covered them and kept them safe Blake did the man of God for forget about that?

"Rita, I don't need you, of all people, to preach to me. I want to keep this short. I don't know what you want but let me tell you what you will get and that is absolutely nothing."

Blake don't believe you could stand there and say you will not let me back into my daughter's lives. You are married with a child on the way. How could you deny me the opportunity to reconnect with my children. They are all I have.

You died 10 years ago and we have moved on. I will not inject you back into our lives just because you decide you want to be resurrected.

What happened to loving kindness and forgiveness Blake. You are the preacher known around the world for ministering love, in loveless places. How can you stand there and take no thought in denying me the chance to have a relationship with my children.

You lost that chance Rita a long time ago. You left us and we didn't even know it. We prayed, we confessed that you were alive but you could not get back to us for some reason. We searched in every way we knew how. The girls were devastated and so was I, but I had to be a strong father for them.

It was me and God and more God than me most times. I grieved so long, I did not know I was grieving. But then one day I seem to waken and breathe again, I could smell again, I could feel again, I could see again. I let the promises of God work within me.

I had preached every Sunday and continued to teach the word but I had not let it do its work inside me. I was not living and believing what I was saying. Yet people were being blessed and lives were being changed.

I don't know how I was able to attend to our children but somehow they grew stronger and became two remarkable young ladies. I now understand what the old timers mean when they talk about leaning on God. I not only leaned on God, I was carried by Him. I loved you Rita and I loved our life together and I loved you as preacher and a woman of God. I was so proud of you and you were so special to the people.

It's funny Blake, you never expressed such admiration all the years we were together. I always felt I was missing mark. I never seemed to measure up to your standards.

Rita I don't want to go back and visit the past. We are dealing with the present and presently you can forget about coming back into our lives. You should just continue living as you have been living. But there is one thing I must ask you, did you turn your back on God like you turned your back on us?

I did not turn my back on anyone, I just set my sights on my purpose and on why I was put on this earth. You remember I use to preach on that a lot, Jeremiah 29:11. I lost my way somehow; my vision I guess, but Katrina, in all its devastation, gave me my life back. I loved my family and I loved

God but I did not love myself. Those girls would not be who they are today if that old Rita stayed in their lives. For that matter, you would not be who you are today.

Rita are you saying you helped God to make things the way they were supposed to be? Please Rita, don't deceive yourself or try to justify your selfish actions.

Look Blake, I want a relationship with my daughters. They are growing up and will soon have lives of their own, I am asking you to give me an opportunity to introduce myself to them. Then let them decide if they want a relationship with me. That is only fair. They can decide for themselves.

I am their father and I will decide for them and my answer is no. I don't want to make things difficult for you. You have made an impressive life here in Washington, but I suspect you had to engage in some deception to keep up your false identity. Did you steal someone's social security number or did you assume someone's identity completely. There were plenty of opportunities given the confusion and mayhem during those horrible days in NO. I will expose you Rita and bring down this fine establishment if you dare to cross me. I don't think the powerful and wealthy of Washington would patronize any establishment run by a liar and a thief.

CHAPTER 13

FINDING A VOICE

A soft knock at the door, aroused Lacy from deep thought. She knew her husband and she knew something had happened to change his mood and his spirits. She could not pinpoint when it happened exactly but she noted the shift sometime during their lunch at the restaurant. Then he goes out in a strange city for a run or walk or something. Esther's voice came shortly after the knock.

Mother can I talk to you?

Sure honey, come in.

I heard dad go out and I was waiting to talk to you. I am really excited about coming here in the fall. But I am concerned about Dexter. I think he wants something more of me and I'm not ready for that.

You are not ready for what? For marriage? For commitment? What?

I'm not ready for any of it. I thought I was but then I see how Dexter was brought up and I see his poor mother. She is so quiet and docile and I don't think she has any choice in how things work in her household between her husband and even her son. If Dexter was exposed to that kind of environment, I don't think he will be any different.

How can you say that Esther, your father is a rather demanding man yet you turned out to be a very compassionate and sensitive person.

I'd know if that would have been the case had we not lost our mother in the way we did. It was all so sudden and it was so painful for such a long time. You become so dependent on God to help you through something like that.

I never really talked to you and Debora about the whole experience, Blake was the only one who shared what happened during that terrible time and I never felt that he really shared it all.

I know dad is the only one in the family that would talk about it but it was always from his perspective. He has never really asked us how we felt or what we remembered. Neither one of us really remembers how our mother looked. We talk about it sometimes but Debora is the one who really is obsessed with know more about our mother and her family.

Now Esther, aren't you being a little hard on your father. When I met your father, his only concern, other than the ministry, was his daughters.

I am not saying he did not care about us or wanted us to be safe. It's just that he never really wanted to deal with our feelings, our hurts, our fears, and our confusion. He acted more like our pastor than our dad. He wanted us to trust God and keep moving on. But we were children, I was eleven and Debora was seven, we needed our dad not a pastor. But that's who dad is and he's never varied from that way of being. But mother you have been wonderful in getting him to be more flexible and less uptight. And now with the babies coming, I think dad will be very different this time around.

Esther, I am sorry we have never talked about what you were feeling. That's something your father and I have in common, we tend not to revisit past events or discuss what happened yesterday.

Is that truly how you want it to be; not to deal with things that may need resolving?

It has worked for us. But as for you and DeBora, you should have felt free to express your feelings, especially if it is about something unresolved.

So how did we get on that, you wanted to talk about you and Dexter. Well, the only thing I will say about that is, you know what to do. I trust your judgment and I trust your faith. You know your father always thought of you as the other preacher in the family. He thinks God is just training you by way of the law. I know you are special and Dexter knows it too. So if he chooses to ignore who you are, then there is your answer.

It is that simple isn't it? As if on cue, the door to their hotel suite opened quietly, Blake wanted his return to the room unnoticed. But his return was anything but unnoticed. In fact, his behavior the entire day screamed for attention.

CHAPTER 14

GOD RULES OVER THE AFFAIRS OF MEN

Rita sat in her driveway but could not remember the drive home or much of anything after Blake left her at the restaurant earlier. It was all a blur except for a clear voice belonging to the man she once loved and a man she once honored as a man of God, a husband, and the father of her children.

"You cannot come back into our daughter's lives. You are dead to them and you will remain that way!" You are dead to me!

Lights on the patio came on, Francios had obviously waiting up. Rita wanted to take her time gathering herself to come in.

Francios was in deep anguish the whole evening but he tried to calm himself by listening to his favorite music and working on the first draft of his book "Art Anyone?" He rehearsed all the "what ifs" concerning his life with Rita — what if they had married, what if they had started a family, what if they had moved back to Paris, what if they had stayed just friends. As he played out the what ifs, the same ending seemed to play out, Rita's past was always resurrected. There was no getting around it, Rita's life in NO was a part of who she was, a mother, a wife, a pastor and a woman that was suppose to change things.

The front door opened slowly and the plank at the front entrance that usually squeaks, to announcing your approach to the hallway, was without sound this time. Francios was determined to give Rita the space to decide when she wanted to see or speak to him. He didn't know what to say but he knew to listen and to comfort. He would do anything to keep the woman he loved who was his heart and soul.

Then out of the silence came her sweet voice that always seemed to have an element of vulnerability.

Francios I'm home, Francois, Fran

I am here my sweet. Come out onto the patio, the moon is waiting for you.

Oh my, it seems to fill the sky, it's what you see on the beach or in the middle of the ocean.

My Rita, it is for you. It's to bring you light even when things seem very dark.

Francois, you are the most wonder non-theologian, theologian I have ever met. Is it that obvious things are somewhat dark for me?

Rita, I am a man that has seen many things, I have encountered many different people and different situations. When you threaten a man's world, his existence, and the essence of which he is, you unleash a mighty force that will do anything to protect and defend that fortress. This Mr. Blake was threatened.

But we are talking about a man that is supposed to be committed to God, not to the things of this world.

That has always been your Achilles heel Rita, your belief in what should be and your denial of what really is. I don't fault you for that, it makes you unique, a visionary and a creative force. But it puts you in place that can lead to great disappointment and deep hurt. I have known this of you and it has caused me to be so careful in my dealings with you. I never wanted to disappoint you but I am human and it happens sometimes.

Francois you have never disappointed or hurt me. You have been nothing but express loving kindness toward me. I have always felt safe with you and that has been so important and comforting to me.

But Blake, in one evening, has managed to disappoint, hurt and take away every level of safety I thought I once had.

He refuses to let me reconnect with my children and he is threatening my existence as a business woman and as a respected person in this community. He wants to destroy me if I make any attempt to inject myself back into my daughters' lives. There was no compassion or feeling and strangely enough, it erased any guilt or doubt about, why I had to leave. I could not breath when he was speaking to me and I remember experiencing that when we were together, he would speak to me in ways that caused me literally to stop breathing.

Rita, what do you want to do, tell me and we will make it happen. This preacher is not invincible. Just as you could not believe how he dismissed you without compassion or feelings, well I don't think those people that follow him would believe it as well.

I don't want to hurt him or his ministry, I just want a relationship with my children.

And that will not happen Rita, if you are waiting on him to realize the right thing to do and do it. He thinks he is right and you are wrong. There is also the matter of your status in his life. You are alive, and he has remarried, you create a messy problem for him as a whole. You cannot arise again.

CHAPTER 15

THE MESSAGE AND THE MESSENGER

Sunday mornings were such rituals in the Blake household. Blake went for a prayer walk/run. The girls selected their Sunday outfits, recognizing they would be scrutinized and critiqued on every aspect of their outer appearance. Lacy, Blake's pregnant wife, had a reprieve, after all she was the wife of a prominent minister, the step mother of two young women and the mother to be of twins. She gained points just for showing up looking quite elegant given her current state of affairs.

Going to Reverend Fauntroy's church in Washington, where Presidents, Heads of State and foreign dignitaries visited was a bit overwhelming for Lacy. But Blake was so sure of his mission and God's call on his life, he was in his element. He was unmoved and totally focused on delivering the message that was for that appointed time. He always knew he had a message not just for the church but for the world.

Lacy I am going for a quick run around the monument, it would be a shame to leave Washington not having done that. I what to see what the hype is all about.

Ok honey, please be mindful of time. I don't want to get there just when you are ready to preach,

I'll be back in plenty of time.

Lacy turned her attention to the Women's Conference Agenda, Reverend Fauntroy's wife shared with her. Lacy looked forward to attending in the coming week since it would be the only time she'd have just for herself.

Suddenly interrupted by knocks on the adjoining, door she allowed the girls to come pouring in with their outfits of choice. They entered with their chatter about the morning service events.

I don't know why I'm so nervous about visiting this church; how many churches have we visited over the years.

DeBora you talk as though you have so many years behind you.

Mother, I feel as though I do. I have shaken so many hands; had so many prayers prayed over me; heard so many sermons and seen so much hypocrisy, yes, I do think I am qualified to say, a lot of experience has been packed into my brief 17 years of living. I'm off to college in the fall, the first step in the pursuit of a medical career and I'll be the sister to a great trail lawyer one day; eventually the sister to twins who will surely follow in dad's path and I'm the daughter of God sent parents. So why wouldn't I thing myself a person that God has given much. And to whom much is given, much is required.

Guys I have pressures that none of you have, not even dad and he's delivering the sermon this morning. I have my future hanging in the balance; do I encourage Dexter or do I let him know there is a purpose for my life and it must be fulfill before I think about a commitment to him.

Esther you are being way too serious, you will certainly be an excellent trail lawyer, the jurors will be putty in your hands.

Girls, come on now, we need to get ready and you know how your dad will come breezing through at the 11th hour wanting us to be ready and waiting on him.

Lacy we need your opinion on the outfits we're wearing this morning, DeBora insisting on input before they retreat to their room.

Well, I think we all should wear green. Esther and Debora, as if on cue said in exasperation… GREEN!

Blake's run around the historic monuments of Washington was all that it was cut out to be. There was a surge of adrenaline inexplicable to the natural senses. You wonder how the most inept person of this democratic system of power could think of themselves as having something worthy of saying. Now Blake knew, it was the intoxication and the deceptiveness of these images of power that seduced men and women in other directions after initially coming to this place with such purpose and vision.

It was interesting how Washington was cohabitated. Within blocks of each other, there was wealth /power and then there was poverty and despair. Blake felt the conversation of yesterday evening wanting to invade his thoughts but it was not coming in... yesterday was yesterday... forgetting those things that are behind.

CHAPTER 16

THE VISITATION

Blake was at his finest at First Bethel of Washington. The congregation responded with resounding approval of his message and of the messenger. There were several members of Congress in the audience and it was rumored that the President slipped into the balcony undetected by those in attendance. If it were so, the President heard a message unedited and unscripted by man.

There was also another visitor unnoticed and undetected by man. He sat on the last row. A journalist that was doing a featured piece on mega ministers and on those so called messengers of God who had masses of people under their influence and control. As Joshua listened to the message, he also observed the people who where spellbound by a speaker who could have lead them off a cliff, if he so desired. Who are these people with this charisma and this gift of speech and words. As a writer, Joshua was particularly sensitive to the power of words and how it can move and transform people, places and things. Those with the gift and power to use words can do great service or do great harm. Over the ages, this has proven true in Jesus, Aristotle, Napoleon, Hitler, FDR, MLK; The man that stood before Joshua seemed to be capable of both.

Joshua did not want to bring out his reporter's note pad and be obvious with his copious note taking but he noted others were writing notes to record the key points of the message. The messenger made this process particularly easy since he announced the seven key points of his message.

Joshua smiled slightly when he thought of his motive for covering the assignment. Owen Blake was from NO and he had come to prominence by literally turning the New Orleans Katrina disaster into a story of victory and triumph. This country loves a great story of victory, in the face of insurmountable obstacles. Katrina and the government's response or lack thereof, to this tragedy, was such a stain on the blotter of this great country called the USA. Blake's story was inspiring, it was overcoming in spite of the loss of his wife, the loss of his church building where he ministered; the loss of hope in a community that had challenges before the storm and the loss of innocence of his two daughter. It was a powerful story and very useful to those who sought exoneration from responsibility and blame.

Joshua listened attentively and he reflected on how Reverend Blake was one of the few who benefited from that New Orleans' hurricane of the century. As he reflected on Blake's fortunes, Joshua could not help but acknowledge he too was a benefactor of Katrina. Settling back in his seat to actually listen to the sermon of a man who's called, in some circles, the people's preacher. His text was on love; how perfect for a man that seemed to feed off of love from people. As the audience became more engaged in the preacher's message, the more the man who stood before them, became riveted. As Joshua looked around, he saw recognizable faces in the audience. The church was known for its powerful membership roster and its who's who visitors. Many expected the pastor of this church, Reverend Fauntroy, to step into the political arena but he seemed to be satisfied in being an orchestrator of politics vs. a player on the field. The sermon was concluding and now they were bringing the guest pastor's family forward. His pregnant wife was introduced along and his two daughters. The daughters were obviously from the wife that was lost in Katrina. As Joshua preceded to slip out the door before the service had concluded, he ran into another person who also had the same exit strategy. She was obviously there in cogneato with dark shades, a floppy hat and Prada sportswear. When she looked up as they both headed for the door, there was a haunting familiarity in her presence.

CHAPTER 17

KNOWING YOUR PURPOSE

Lacy was excited about getting away from Blake and the girls for the morning. They had been in Washington for five days and every moment seemed to be filled with someone else's agenda, Blake's invite to the Capitol; Esther's visit to Georgetown's campus; Debora's visit to the Washington's inner city community services.

It was invigorating to attend a sessions of the Woman's Conference at Reverend Fauntroy's church. Elizabeth, Reverend Fauntroy's wife was a warm and kind woman. She had been so considerate and thoughtful every since they arrived in Washington. She was a wonderful person but definitely under serious control by her husband. But there was a strength within this woman. It was only looking for a way to unfold. As Lacy approached the church, her prayers were as always, for God to use her and show her anyone that was to be her specific assignment in the space she found herself. That was her prayer when she first met Blake and it was through that prayer that she knew he would be her husband.

Lacy reflected on the invitation Elizabeth extended for her to say a few words at the beginning of the conference but she declined. It was always Lacy's desire to remain a quiet presence and it seemed to be reinforced as Blake's wife. He had a co-pastor wife and it seemed to have been a challenge for him to share that spotlight particularly if the other person was such a natural at it.

There was already a sizeable crowd when she arrived. The attendees were diverse, there were well dressed individuals, those in jeans, the church members; the young the old; black women, white women, Spanish, Asian. It is was so different from a Conference in Atlanta. However, Lacy smiled because the church dynamics she observed never seemed to change no matter the church or the location.

Elizabeth, it's so good to see you. It's good to be here this morning.

It's good to see you. Let's go back to the office so you can meet some of the speakers for the morning session.

The church building was impressive; the offices were as pristine as that of a corporate entity. It was a measure of success for a church structure, to look and feel like its corporate counterpart. A Fortune 500 and mega churches had more things in common than most people would image.

Lacy was ushered into a lovely office with an adjoining conference room. She was struck by the impressiveness of the women sitting around the conference table. These women were striking, they didn't have to say anything, and their presence was enough to conclude they were women of substance.

Ladies let me introduce First Lady Lacy Blake from Atlanta, she and her husband Owen Blake are here in Washington for the week. Reverend Blake gave the message this past Sunday and a riveting one it was.

Good morning ladies, I am so looking forward to the sessions this morning. I read the title of some of your messages and I was intrigued.

Well we are intrigued by you Mrs. Blake, you are one of the few pastor wives of mega churches that is functioning quietly in the background. Most mega church wives seem compelled to come to the forefront even if it really isn't their calling. The woman chiming in with her personal observation was a pastor from a traditional denomination who had experienced sexism and racism of the harshest form from the church brethren.

I never thought about co-pastoring with my husband. I know where I flow comfortably and I believe it is a blessing for everyone concerned.

I like that and it's the way we should operate as wives and women of God. Just know where you fit and stay with it no matter what forces try to pull you from it. Elizabeth made that pronouncement as if she were convincing herself. The worship in the sanctuary was filtering into the conference room signaling it was time to make their way to the sanctuary. Lacy was surprised when they asked her to pray before they proceeded but even more amazed at how comfortably she responded to the request. When she completed the prayer, Lacy was certain she had done what she was appointed to do for that time.

CHAPTER 18

WALKING IN THE SHADOW

Esther was anxious to return to Georgetown's campus, being free to explore without an agenda. When she came the first time, there were several places she made mental note to return to when there was more time. The running path was one of those places, as well as the Christian Student Center and an art plaza where local artists' have their art pieces on display. The Christian Center was the first stop. It was a warm friendly environment and an obvious hang-out for students of all persuasions. That was curious given it was the Christian Student Center. But when she stepped into an area with a bistro; starbucks, New Orleans flare, she understood the attraction. Students came for conversation, discount gourmet coffee, tea, juice and multimedia toys. There were headphones so everyone could engage in their personal preference of entertainment or distraction. It was midmorning and there was an ample number of students occupying the space. It was indicative of its popularity as the day progressed. Esther sat down to take in the experience of the space she'd call home in a few months. She closed her eyes and took a deep breath, reflecting on a life in Washington D.C. Away from her father's enormous shady, away from the many things that seemed to restrict her passion and purpose.

Unnoticed by Esther, at the doorway of the Christian Student Center stood a woman who'd just completed her run. She stopped short of the café area observing the young lady who was clearly a visitor. There Rita stood within 20 feet of her oldest daughter and the recognition of this young woman caused a rush of blood to her head and weak knees.

Esther, she whispered, at the same time Blake's voice came flooding back "you cannot come back into our daughters' lives, you are dead to them and you will stay that way."

CHAPTER 19

TELLING THE STORY

Joshua had an impressive home office, designed specifically to accommodate his writing habits. He needed lots of light, organized space, and plants, lots of plants. However he still did most of his quality writing in the bedroom, filled with books, a sound system and a large bay window. Old row houses in Washington were filled with character and unique qualities. The house had gone through at least four cycles of ownership, which represented the transitions experienced, by the city. The house was built in 1936 just after the area was starting to define itself as a town of diplomats. It was filled with hardwood floors, an impressive built in china cabinet, a porcelain fireplace, a full English basement, and a lively garden in the backyard, of sorts. The houses where connected in the front which is why they were called row houses but the back of the houses had distinct separation. Joshua loved the back of the house, it was a cozy setting and quite serene. His last girlfriend convinced him to string white Christmas lights around the back porch and keep them up year-round. He was not keen on the idea but even after her exit, Joshua maintained the lights and enjoyed the soft atmosphere it set when he sat out in the evening with his wine and his books.

Writing this featured story on Owen Blake was going to be an interesting fleet in balancing suspicions about all televangelist and personal admiration for this particular man. This man's story paralleled his story in several ways. Hurricane Katrina was horrific but this man, Owen Blake, triumphed in the midst of the storm, so to speak. He was a local preacher who would have remained so, had he not been cater pillared into the spotlight by prominent state and national officials captured by his charisma and his story of a wife who perished in the storm and left with two little girls who needed their mother. Joshua's story also turned upward in the midst of the Katrina tragedy. He was close to throwing his life away before he came to NO. He wanted to end it all, yet found himself helping a woman who was obviously not use to being a state of helplessness. While traveling with her to Houston, on that endless bus trip, he came to realize what was blocking his writing and blocking his life's progress for that matter. He wondered many times whatever happened to that woman but he would always remember what happened to him. After leaving that strange woman in Houston, he came back to NO and Joshua came alive, he was resurrected. He captured the horrors of Katrina from the perspective of people who believed in God's power over all things. Many of these believers did not leave the city when evacuation was mandated. They were confident in their God's protection and in help ultimately coming from the government e.g., city, state or Federal. But it did not come as expected, they were on their own and their own was not strong enough to withstand everything that came. Joshua saw it first hand, those that were suppose to protect, didn't. There was a strange sense of power in knowing that the perceived powerful source was not so powerful. He felt powerful as one individual helping another individual secure safety. He helped that woman on the bus, that woman that was strong yet weak and vulnerable.

Joshua looked at the time and realized the morning had been spent, reflecting on the past and not focused on the article that was due in two days. He had decided not to do any interviews for the article but rather do some objective research about this man who experienced an extraordinary rise in ministry and influence in the midst of great tragedy. The subject of Hurricane Katrina was filled with immeasurable destruction and great suffering. However, there were stories of victory and resurgence, which were yet to be told. Reverend Owen Blake was one of those stories and the author of the article was yet another.

CHAPTER 20

WHERE HE LEADS

Rita was filled with emotions and regrets of the past and of the present. Her daughters were young ladies and she missed the most precious years of their lives. Now she was just some strange woman in their lives. Her husband wanted her to stay dead and her lover was immune to the pain and suffering that defined most of her life.

The restaurant had not been high on her priority over the last several weeks but the business was going through a critical period. They were looking to expand into Canada, so it was important that she be focused on the direction of the restaurant and sit future. But her daughter would be going to school less than one mile away from her, how could she breath the same air and see the same things and stay focused as if everything remained the same.

Ms. Rita a very nice note came from Congressman Wade's office this morning to thank us for the lunch and the great service the Monet shared with his guest.

That's very lovely Amanda, you were very instrumental in making everything perfect for the Congressman and his guests.

Thanks Ms. Rita, but may I say, things seemed to have changed since that day of the lunch. You stopped the personal customer service spot checks, we are all so use to. You stopped doing the walk around management. You stopped being the one who always knew the mood and temperament of all the staff including temporary help. We miss you Ms. Rita.

Amanda only you would notice and you are right, my world did change that day or shall I say my life was resurrected. You have heard of worlds colliding, well my world collided with another, that day. My past and present worlds crashed and it made more of a bang than I would have ever thought.

Ms. Rita, I don't understand, what happened?

I can't or maybe I'm not ready to talk about it now but I will and I must at some point in time.

For right now, my plan is to go to New York for several months to secure the operations there and make plans to move into Canada, So I am really going to need you to be Rita Jr, in every way possible.

You are leaving me in charge, I don't know what to say. I should be excited but I'm feeling sad. Amanda you are a Bible reader and I think you should know the passage that says, everything must change, and nothing stays the same.

Yes, it in the old testament. I can't think of exactly where. Amanda responded hesitantly. Rita spoke in a whisper, it's in Ecclesiastes.

CHAPTER 21

THE MISSION

Owen Blake and his family returned to Atlanta from their Washington D.C. journey but Blake knew they had not returned to their life as before. His wife was well aware of the change. The girls were so absorb in their lives, they noticed very little that did not directly affect them. Blake was not a patient man but he seemed even more impatient upon their return.

Owen, honey is there something going on or did something happen in Washington that we need to talk about. I've let this cloud hover over us thinking you would come around but things don't seem to be getting better.

Look Sweetie, I know I've been distracted recently but it will all work itself out. Just trust and believe that it will.

I do trust Owen but I know you are not opening up to me and I can't agree with you on things working itself out if I don't know what is going on. Look, we will be having the babies in less than three months and I need my husband to be fully focused and engaged. So let me know now if that is not going to be the case.

Sweetie I have never, seen you rise up so strongly before. I guess this is what pregnant woman do, protecting their babies.

Owen, I always felt your protection of me and us but now I feel a little uncovered.

I'm sorry you feel that way. Look there is a major trip on the calendar, which has been scheduled since last year. You know I am committed to making this trip to Africa, for the outreach ministry. I did not reschedule because it fits perfectly into everything else that's going on. It's before you are due to deliver and its before Esther and Debora go off to school.

Owen, I feel you should cancel that trip. I think there is too much going on for you to take it.

I cannot cancel at this point. Agenda's have been established and the pastor's in Nigeria are counting on this visit.

The days leading up to the trip were filled with tension and silence in the Blake household, lots of silence. Blake spoke very little, the girls were in their rooms or out and Lacy sat in the nursery looking around, listening to classical music which Blake never really enjoyed. He always that opera was like someone crying. So listening to opera was reserved for those times when Blake was not around or not in listening distance. It was funny how Lacy stopped going to operas and to symphony concerts once she married Owen. As Lacy reflected on that area was absent in her life. Thoughts of Owen's first wife, for some reason, rose up in her consciousness. Owen rarely spoke of his first wife, which is still very painful for the girls but when he speaks of her, it seem to be in a voice of regret. He once mentioned how, she loved art and how she wanted them to visit art galleries. He never went because he said he considered the activity like watching paint dry. It was interesting the type of wives Owen chose. They were women who had great enjoyed and delighted in the things he so detested. As Lacy's mind, wander over all the things that had never been spoken or discussed, the awareness of the shift in atmosphere within the Blake household became more pronounced. As if an echo from out Lacy's little corner of the universe, Owen's voice penetrated her thoughts.

Lacy, are you packing the shirts I like to wear?

Yes. I packed them but I thought you may want shirts that are more casual.

No, I'll wear the collarless most of the time. It lets the people know I'm a minister and ready to pray with them on the spot at anytime. This is going to be a long trip and I tell you Lacy, I've never felt this way about a trip. I believe it will change the direction of our ministry. There was a silence that filled the room after he made that statement. It was as thou it were a prophetic word.

The sound of DeBora yelling from the bottom stairwell, jilted them both back to the present space they shared.

Dad, Dad, Dad are you up there? the package from the school arrived.

DeBora, why did I bothered having intercoms installed throughout the house, if everyone still insist on yelling.

Debora, bolting up the stairs in two step strides, entered the room as though a trumpet had sounded.

Hey mom, dad, the orientation package from NO state just arrived. They even have several roommate options.

Roommate options? Lacy asked with some levity.

Yes, options. They know if women are to share the same space in harmony, there must be some degree of repoire.

So what happened to the scripture that says be peaceable with all men.

Yea dad but there are different levels of peace. There's silent peace, rebellious peace, bulling peace.

Ok I get your very worldly message. So you have definately decided on NO state.

Yes, Dad I thought that was all settled. I don't know why you want me to stay here in Atlanta. I will be in your hair, and I'll be an evolving scholar that will need room to explore and grow.

That's part of my conflict, I'm not fully persuaded on this business of exploring.

Dad, how will you know and more important how will I know that all the teachings and the prayers and the love are more than enough to cover and protect me in all circumstances. Besides, I really want to go back to NO again. I feel there is something there for me to experience and receive.

DeBora, yours dad and I love you. We want you to go through your college years with great success. But give us time to get use to releasing you. Your father and I know you are a young woman of substance, good character and you know the source of your strength. By the time we ship you off to school in a couple of months, we'll be on board. We promise, don't we honey?

Yes, yes Lacy, I promise. Now DeBora, I don't have time to go over this package so sit down with your sister and your mom and make sure you have all the important information reviewed and acted on.

So when I get back, we'll go over everything and get things in the mail. Is that a deal.

Ok dad, I accept my assignment. But I don't know how much time Esther will have to help me? She has her own orientation stuff to deal with.

Well I think by now, Esther has a handle on all that, she's done it a time or two.

Dad, I think you should talk to Esther just the same. She may be having some anxiety over this move.

Well thanks Ms. counselor, I'll do that.

Guys, let's get ready for lunch, I invited, the ladies ministry leaders over for a light meal. I felt they were floundering a bit, so I thought some focused time may help.

Esther found herself in a mall, alone. A place she would never be unless there was a compelling purpose. DeBora, told her about a lady she met in Washington at a street vendor stand. Leave it to DeBora to strike up an instant conversation. The stand had Historically Black College memorabilia, so she saw NO state T shirts and caps and the rest was history. Apparently, the lady was from NO but moved to Atlanta after the storm. Now she travels to some of the major black populated cities to generate money and expand her customer base for her business. She said she had a kiosk in a mall in Atlanta. So now, Esther was reluctantly but anxiously going to visit that mall. She told DeBora she remembered our mother and father and their ministry. It was strange that DeBora seemed apprehensive about following up with the woman. DeBora was always secretly trying to find out more about their mother and her family. Yet here was a possible source of information and it was dropped on Esther like an unwanted child.

What did she know about their mother, what was she like, did she really preach better than their father, was she pretty, was she funny and smart, was she … There were dozens of questions running through Esther's head as if this woman was a close friend and confidant of her mother's. But based on Debora's assessment, she either knew their parents from a distance or she just heard of them.

The kiosk stand was directly in front of her. She stood at a distance for a moment to observe the activity and to have a look at the women that said she knew Arrita Blake.

There was a woman that appeared to be serving customers. She was full in figure and appeared to be disabled in one arm. The movement of her right arm appeared restricted but it did not seem to affect her effort to manage the kiosk. Esther smiled as she sized up the woman remembering how her father always commented on her keen sense of observation. In the spirit, he said I had a mature sense of discernment. DeBora on the other hand had zeal which caused her toys jump into things before she checked it out. However, with this woman, DeBora did not seem anxious to charge in. In fact, she felt the woman was patronizing, her so a sale could be made.

As Esther approached the kiosk, she observed scriptures written around the bottom of the cart. Ashes to gladness, weakness to strength, poverty to riches. The woman was busy with a customer so Esther had an opportunity to inspect her merchandise. She spotted Howard University memorabilia and ponder if she should buy anything. Suddenly the woman was directly in front of her asking if she could help her find something.

Esther, realizing she was a bit nervous, paused and then asked, do you do any business in the Washington D.C. area. The woman quickly responded.

Yes, in fact I was there several weeks ago.

My family and I were also there several weeks ago. In fact, I'll be moving there in several months.

So what takes you there.

I'll be going to Howard's law school.

That's great and I wish you well in your future endeavors. Would you like some Howard University memorabilia to get you ready for your new place?

I was just thinking about that but I noticed you also have quite a bit of NO merchandise. I'm originally from NO although I lived in Atlanta most of my life.

So you moved here after the storm.

How did you know. It was the way you said it. Like there is a missing piece and you are still looking for it.

How did you conclude all that from what I just said.

Because I get a lot of customers from NO and after all these years, I can tell those that left NO after Katrina, never to return and those that are still attached to NO storm or no storm. You sound like those that left never to return,. But it was your parents that brought you to Atlanta so you have some attachment to NO because you were abruptly taken from that place.

Actually, it was my father who moved us here. My mother died in the storm.

I am so sorry. I lost several relatives but not a mother. Not a mother.

Do you remember all that happened?

It's strange even though I was young, you'd think I'd remember something but the whole thing is a complete blank. So much so, I can't even remember my mother's face.

You're not allow young lady. I could have easily erased all the memories of that time but I needed to remember to assure we people never forget what can happen when you trust solely in government or some other earthy power.

So you are a Christian? My dear I am a believer in God and Jesus his son. If not I would be crazy or dead by now.

Ms. . . .

Call me Patrice

Ms. Patrice, the reason I came to your business today was because my sister met you in Washington and in the course of your conversation, she understood you to say, you may have known my mother and father in NO.

They were both pastors at a small church in St. Charles parish.

And what were their names?

Arrita and Owen Blake.

Yes, I remember talking with your sister. She was so lively and animated but when I told her that I knew of your parents and your mother in particular, she practically ran from my stand.

Please forgive my sister, she has been seeking answers about our mother and she has been led down a number of dead end streets. I think she was a little spooked about you saying you knew our mother. Our mother was never found and I think that seems to keep our wounds from totally healing.

So what does your father tell you about your mother and those days during the storm.

That's the problem, he doesn't really talk about it in detail including the particulars about our mother.

Isn't your father the pastor over that mega church here in Atlanta.

Yes madam he is. So did you know my mother?

CHAPTER 22

NEW BEGINNINGS

Rita actually found herself looking forward to her temporary relocation to NY. It would be a distraction from the heart wrenching fact that her husband, the father of her children wanted her never to enter the lives of their daughters. If only those words would stop playing over and over in her head. "as far as we are concerned, you are dead to us and it will stay that way."

On some level, Rita accepted this pronouncement as punishment for what she'd done. She abandoned her marriage and her children and she was living with a man that was not her husband. However, Rita knew she carried around a matter more burdensome than those she quickly acknowledged. She had walked away from God and the call for her life. She was a preacher and a pastor. Rita knew those things as well as she knew her name but she also felt she was losing her identify and she had to get out.

However, since Blake's visit, things had changed completely. Francios noticed the change but said nothing. He was not a Christian but he was a spiritual man. He recognized that there was a higher power but he had no clue about having a personal relationship with God. It was not by happenstance that he was so different from Blake. In physical makeup Blake was African American, Francios was European; in spirituality Blake was a Christian pastor, Francios had no religious affiliations, Blake was from a modest background, Francios lived a life of wealth and privilege all his life.

In taking inventory, Rita recognized her extreme makeover but now Rita the woman designed of God, had been resurrected. She was lost and now she is found.

Rita, darling.

Yes Francios.

I think we have secured a lovely apartment for you in NY overlooking the park and there are other nice amenities on the property. It's available for six months but I told them we wouldn't need it for that long.

Rita heard the question that was not a question. How long will you be gone?

Francios, I told you we did not have to get such a fancy place. I'll be working at the restaurant most of the time so it's just going to be a place to sleep and talk to you.

Darling I'm not having you slumming in NY so that's settled. Now how long should I make the lease.

Why don't we keep it for six months but I should be back before then. Just in case I need to make several visits back once, we transition with the new chef.

Rita, I feel our world shifting and I can't do anything about it. I never thought we would separate but here we are.

Francios you saved my life when my world not only shifted it was turned upside down. When we met 10 years ago, I thought I'd have to operate without breathing. Trust me my darling, you're safe in this shift.

· · · · ·

DeBora was looking forward to living in NO. It was like something was waiting for her there. It was curious how no one except her sister, was excited about this new adventure and her new life in NO. When Esther went off to college her first year, there was some much anticipation, but her Dad seemed almost relieved that his travel schedule conflicted with her plans to leave earlier than initially planned. When they offered her the opportunity to stay on campus weeks before most of the student body would be arriving, she knew it was a perfect plan to get into her NO roots before classes started.

The people at the church where Blake was pastor and where her mother co pastor, were making extraordinary plans for her to come and visit before she started school. They were so excited about pastor Blake's daughter coming home. Technically it was not really coming home to the church they attended as children, since it was destroyed in the flood. But it was the church legacy that was never destroyed.

Her father did not know the degree to which DeBora reached out to the church, but there was something that she needed to do for her mother and for herself.

Esther, do you think Lacy is ok with us both leaving at the same time?

If she was ok with Dad going to Africa before the babies arrived, I don't think she'll have a problem with us flying the nest.

Esther, I's worried about Lacy, I don't think Dad is very sensitive to how she feels. Sometimes the ministry seems to be all consuming in his life. Don't think she wanted him to take the trip to Africa.

Lacy is fine, she just needs to stand up to Dad more or put her foot down when he starts going off the deep end. I think the Africa trip, as important as it was, could have been postponed.

I don't think our mother was as accommodating as Lacy, from what I hear. She spoke with authority and most people, including Dad listened.

So Ms. DeBora, what makes you such the expert on Mom and Dad?

Esther, every since we met the lady in the mall in Washington, I can't help thinking about our Mom. She had such an impact on that lady and obviously on many others. I don't understand why Dad does not talk about her more and I don't think it is out of respect for Lacy. Lacy, always showed us how much she wanted us to know our mother, even though Dad seemed to block it.

Girls, how is packing coming along?

Hey mommy, how are you? We were just talking about you.

DeBora, what's wrong? You always make me nervous when you're this reserved and accommodating.

Nothing's wrong, I guess, we're somewhat sad about leaving you and Dad and twins.

Well you aren't leaving forever and we will be visiting you both, when schedules permit. Too bad you girls aren't in the same city, that would make visiting very efficient. But it's no surprise you girls are covering both ends of the east coast, the northern and southern regions.

Have you heard from Dad this morning?

No, I haven't and he usually calls around this time but I know the ministry stops are packed so he probably went to bed early.

. . . . .

We're going down, brace yourselves for impact. The message from the pilot was the last communication picked up from the plane carrying Reverend Owen Blake and his missionary team of approximately twenty-five people. That was the information communicated to the local transportation authorities, who informed the Federal Transportation Authorities (FTA) in Washington. The local officials were unfamiliar with a tragic event of this nature and unsure of proper protocol. The FTA advised the local authorities to immediately restrict further communications until international officials were on the scene.

"Did you know this Pastor Blake?" That was the question being whispered at the command center of the airport where the plane was scheduled to arrive. There was an obvious distinction between those who knew Reverend Owen Blake and those who knew about him. Those knowing him were visibly impacted by the news.

Lacy felt a heaviness in the air as the day progressed and no word from her husband. To pass the time, she went into the office, where she rarely spent much time, because of Owen's clutter. There were a number of people she wanted to send notes to from their D.C. trip. Everyone one was so kind from Reverend Fauntroy's church and his wife was such an angel. There was also a rather strange connection with the restaurant owner in Georgetown. It was very kind of her to open her home and her restaurant to Esther. It was odd that she did not want the offer mentioned to Blake. It was rare for people to offer kindness in secret, especially those who are well connected.

The evening wore on and still no word from Blake. When the girls asked about hearing from their father, it was with deep faith she offered up a lighthearted response about how he's so focused during trips like this one, he forgets all about his family back home. She was obviously convincing because they proceeded to attend to their agenda's like packing and organizing for their impending moves.

It was unusual to hear a car in the driveway at 11:30 p.m. but she heard several cars on the property and cars doors shutting. In the course of taking a deep breath, she heard the doorbell ring. The camera monitor reflected several people of whom she knew standing at the door. There was Jack Slate, the Assistant Pastor who always thought he was the pastor; John Clayton a quiet thoughtful businessman whom Blake respected highly and Charlotte, Owen's personal assistant. They all stood huddle together with solemn expressions and glaring eyes. Lacy refused to panic or allow feelings of dread flood her thoughts as she answered the door.

Pastor Slate step through the door first, then Charlotte and then John.

"First Lady we know it's late but we wanted to come over to share with you a phone call we received earlier this evening about Pastor and the missionary team." Lacy was very silent and knew not to speculate on what was the reason for their visit. The embassy in Lagos informed us that Blake's plane did not arrive as scheduled and they have not made contact in several hours. They cannot confirm the status but they are concluding that the plane has gone done. Now that can mean a number of things. They may have set down safely in a place where there is no radio contact. We must believe that and nothing else unless we hear something different.

Lacy, heard what was being said but it was like being in fog with everything blurry and unclear. The girls had entered the room and surmised that something was wrong. DeBora, was the first to yell out, it's Dad isn't it? Esther with her calm demur stood quietly waiting for a response. Lacy, open her arms to the girls and they immediately melted in her embrace. "Girl's Daddy's plane has gone missing". We don't know what has happened but we know what we have to do. Esther, who her father said would be a preacher, by way of her law degree, spoke with such conviction. " We that dwell in the secret place of the most high shall mount up as wings of eagle, we shall not faint". Dad always quoted that passage when he was in a battle. So now I know about being in a battle.

CHAPTER 23

AWAKEN

Ms. Moore this is Lacy Blake, I hope you remember me, we met at your restaurant not long ago. Rita was taken back from the call on several levels. She was aware of the tremendous loss this woman was feeling from losing her husband and having to go through the loss so publicly. She was also the " mother" of two girls grieving over their father. Rita followed the details in the paper, Owen Blake's plane crashed and all aboard had parished.

Rita was also in so much conflict over the situation. Knowing her girls were in complete anquish and knowing they did not need yet another shock in their lives by announcing she was their mother.

Yes of course I remember you. How are you Mrs. Blake, please accept my deepest sympathy.

Thank you Ms. Moore, it has been very difficult but there are a lot of people that needed me to be strong. Including these two babies that want to come soon and my girls that are young women going off on their own. Which is why I'm calling you. Esther will be coming to Washington in the next several weeks and I would like your assistance in helping her adjust to the area. What I mean is, if you could show Esther some of the highlights of Washington. You are so well connected in the area and I think it would help Esther through this tough time to have some social outlets. She knows some people already in the area but she may need new people in her life.

I would be honored to show Esther the city but there is a slight problem, I'm currently in NY. I'm dealing with some staff changes in my NY restaurant and preparing to open a new property in Canada. But then you don't want to hear about all my little business affair.

Oh no, I hear a very busy woman and I don't think my request exactly fits into what's happening with you.

Nonsense, I'm delighted you thought of me and I may not be able to personally host Esther but I have one better. You may remember my assistant Amanda. Yes I do, she was so gracious when we were at the restaurant. She made us feel so comfortable and special. My husband mentioned her even when we got back to Atlanta. She sent us a kind note when we got back home. I intended to correspond with her but events over took those plans.

Well my proposal is that Amanda, who is a wonderful, Godly woman, make herself available to Esther. I know Amanda would love to host her and get away from my ongoing demands from NY.

I'm so grateful Ms. Moore, that sounds great, I'll get back with you on all her contact information but I can give you her mobile number now. She'll be living near the campus, in a townhouse with several other law students. I think the street name is Randolph. But I'll get back with you on the exact address. I'm familiar with the area and it's in the heart of the city. For now, I'll pass the information to Amanda. Now is Esther coming to Washington alone? No, A young man who was very close to Owen is accompanying her. In fact Owen treated him more like a son than his executive assistant. He was with Owen in Africa but he was a leg ahead of all of Owen's stops making sure things were organized the way Owen wanted them. He is having a very rough time with being spared and all the others are gone. This trip will help him as well.

Lacy I look forward to hearing from you and thank you for thinking of me and allowing me to support you in this very small way. Please take care of yourself, no I believe the truth is, you should take no care.

I somehow knew there was something deep within you Ms. Moore. We'll be in touch.

Both women somehow struggled with ending the conversation but they both finally stop talking. Rita continued to hold the phone to her ear awhile after the conversation had ended. Then she reflected on the irony of what just happened. Mrs Blake speaking to Mrs. Blake about their daughter. She wanted to fly back to Washington, that day but she knew from experience that only time was the way out of the webs that had been weaved.

Old things must pass away and resurrection awaits in the morning.

The End

www.ingramcontent.com/pod-product-compliance
Lightning Source LLC
Chambersburg PA
CBHW072011170626
46813CB00005B/2110